Fiery Love

Curvy & Decadent, Volume 1

Dee James

Published by Dee James, 2024.

Also by Dee James

Curvy & Decadent
Fiery Love
Cheesy Love
Spicy Love
Crazy Love
Curvy Love
Married Love

Watch for more at https://authordeejames.substack.com/about.

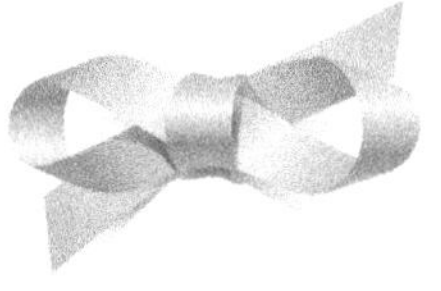

#1

Pari

"Pari, come down, dinner is ready. We're waiting."

I sighed before closing the spicy office romance I'd been reading in my room. Time to go down for dinner. It was the third time I heard my mom announce dinner was ready, and from experience, I knew this was the last call before she'd march into my room to yell right in my face. Knowing her, she was entirely capable of murder and more.

Quickly finger combing my long, silky hair, I ran down the stairs towards the kitchen, abruptly coming to a dead stop. My heart stuttered before galloping at full speed. I felt my mouth turn dry and my eyes widened in shock and awe. Absently, I registered my body's strange reaction; all for the man standing in the middle of the kitchen.

I looked at the tall, handsome man in jeans and a button-down shirt, who also looked vaguely familiar. My gaze was automatically pulled to his piercing gray eyes before my eyes took in his sharp nose, neatly trimmed beard, and his unsmiling lips that gave him a rugged edge.

He was a piece of art. If I had my art supplies right now, I'd have attempted a sketch. My eyes finally moved away from his face, tracing his wide shoulders and muscular frame with curiosity and awe.

Being plus-sized and curvy, it was quite rare for me to feel small. Yet, that's exactly how I felt now—small and delicate—in front of this familiar stranger. Shivering, I felt butterflies swarm my belly when I noticed him looking at me with his stormy, brooding eyes.

That's when my eyes took in the frown that filled his face. Ah, what a sunny personality! Pursing my lips, I barely stopped myself from rolling my eyes at the scowl that didn't seem to recede from his perfect face.

"Oh, thank God, you came down before the apocalypse."

I averted my gaze from the scowling man toward my mom. Thankfully, with her usual sass, she drew me out of my unabashed staring, saving me from doing or saying something stupid.

"Mom!" I glared at the tiny woman who looked a decade younger than her forty-six years. In fact, with our similar build and looks, people often mistook us for sisters.

"Don't *mom* me. I've been yelling for the past twenty minutes. As you can see, we have a very special guest today for dinner and I wanted you to join us on time for once."

I narrowed my eyes when my mom turned towards the handsome man, throwing him an affectionate smile. *Who was this guy? Why did he look so familiar, and why was Mom all smiles?*

"Honey, come over," she addressed me before turning towards Mr. Sunshine once again. "Neil will be here any moment. You already met Navin when he joined Caltech last month, and this is his sister, Pari. You remember her, don't you?"

Noticing Mr. Sunshine's eyes narrowing at me, I tightened my lips. Apparently, I'd already met the handsome man? No way! I'd remember his good looks and his grumpy attitude. Both were hard to miss.

When he noticed my reaction, his lips quirked slightly, making my heart miss a beat. What the hell! This man might look like a model, but that wasn't the reason my pulse was jumping. I've met a lot of good-looking people in my life, and I've never had this strange reaction before.

"Oh, and sweetie, this is Aunty Mia's son, Zain." Mom finally turned towards me once again after being Ms. Congeniality.

I felt my eyes widen. *Zain? Aunt Mia and Uncle Armaan's adopted son, Zain?* My dark eyes swung to my mom, who nodded with a smile. Uncle Armaan was my dad's bestie, and this was their adopted son. Oh! No wonder he looked familiar. Of course, I'd seen him during my childhood.

My dad, Neil Grover, was a techie billionaire to the outside world. For us, he was the perfect husband and dad first. He had three besties from high school: Uncle Arjun, Uncle Armaan, and Uncle Rahul. Uncle Rahul, who was the Minister of External Affairs, lived in the capital city of Delhi, the other two lived near our place in Bangalore.

I remember Aunt Mia and Uncle Armaan had brought Zain home when he'd been a teenager. Unlike their biological son, who was closer to my age, Zain was older. I'd been very young when Zain had joined his new family, and within a few years, he'd gone abroad for college. As far as I could remember, Zain kept to himself mostly, not even attending family events or gatherings much.

Looking at the huge, muscular man with a beard, I couldn't believe this was the same once lanky boy I vaguely remember meeting. Only his eyes were the same, with the same grave expression he'd had all those years ago. No wonder he looked familiar.

"Hi," I waved quickly, unable to stop the blush that crept up my neck. Damn! The embarrassment quickly vanished when I saw Zain nod once. No hello, not even a smile. How rude!

Tossing my hair behind my shoulder, I fumed before walking to the formal dining room, that had an enormous ten-seat table. Just as I finished setting the table on one side, my dad walked in, looking handsome as ever.

"Darling, did you make anything for us today?"

"Hi, Dad." I smiled before continuing, "Not today; although I can whip up some instant dessert for you if you'd like that."

"Don't bother, sweetheart. It's your mom who has the sweet tooth." He grinned at Mom, who'd followed us in before looking at me with a tender expression. "I presume you met Zain already?"

"Mm-hmm." I nodded solemnly, hoping my eyes didn't betray the strange, unsettling feelings I've been experiencing ever since I walked into the kitchen.

My dad nodded as the four of us sat down for dinner.

Zain

Finally, I could sit down. A second longer, and my control could have snapped. Frowning, I filed that thought away, unhappy with anything that threatened to tip my control.

After living in the States for more than a decade, I'd come to India to move closer to my parents. A couple of projects interested me, to be honest, but I was also really looking forward to spending time with my family.

Uncle Neil and my adopted father, Armaan, were best buds since their high school days. Over the years, Uncle Neil and Aunt Tanya became family. When they knew I was home, they'd invited me for a welcome home dinner. I'd naively assumed I'd have a pleasant evening with the couple.

Instead, it felt like my entire world had shifted. My body, mind, and soul imploded when my eyes landed on the most gorgeous and curvy little angel with full lips and long hair. Pari! An apt name. It meant the face of an angel in Hindi.

When she'd walked into the room, my breath had stopped for a few seconds too long. I'd felt a whoosh in my ears and my eyes refused to look away from her captivating form. I couldn't help but notice her perfect curves and glowing skin.

With her curvy hourglass figure, she awakened my body with an ease that left me feeling stunned. Frankly, it had been a few years since my body had shown interest in the opposite sex. After constantly dating power-hungry women who wanted light, no-commitment relationships, I'd been bored.

To most women, my last name and wallet were the star attractions. That I looked good and had a thick dick were added bonuses. When my previous fling ended with my so-called best friend going at it with the girl, I gave up entirely. Not because it hurt me, but because I didn't even care to stop them. I'd assumed I was completely done with women and sex. Clearly, my body and heart were now proving me wrong.

Seated opposite to Pari, I couldn't help but stare at her huge eyes and full lips. Despite her casual dress and bare face, she looked stunning. She had an ethereal beauty that couldn't be achieved by surgery or cosmetics.

Usually, I'm not someone who believes in hearts, flowers, soulmates, and all that. I'm too jaded for all that crap, but looking at the girl who was trying not to glance my way and failing, I was tempted to believe love like that existed.

I'd have continued to stare at Pari but her father's hand on my shoulder brought me out of the strange mood. Clearing my throat awkwardly, I barely bit back an apology for staring at his daughter. "Sorry, I was lost in my thoughts." My voice felt coarse and unused. Well, I've never been one for words and I wasn't about to get chatty now.

"Sweetie, do you want some more curry?" Tanya asked me with a twinkle in her eyes, as if she knew where my attention had been all this while. I flushed with embarrassment, hoping I didn't give her any ideas. Over the years, I've seen my dad and uncles often groan when the 'Matchmaking TinTin' came into play.

"Yes, please. Thank you for having me over. Everything's delicious."

"Something I had no part in." She answered with a chuckle. I tried not to grin; Aunt Tanya's burning skills were legendary and to this day, we all took care never to let her near a stove.

"So, are you moving back this time? Been a long stint abroad, isn't it? It's been, what? Eight years? Nine?" Neil inquired, spooning some food onto his plate.

"A little more than that. Unlike my previous rushed visit, I'm here for a while this time. Mom and Dad are keen to have me around." As always, the minute I spoke about my adopted parents, affection seeped into my voice unconsciously. They meant everything to me. If they hadn't gotten me out of that hellhole all those years ago...

"You're an architect, right?"

I tried not to react when I heard Pari's soft voice. My thoughts immediately scattered, and for a few seconds, my mind turned blank. Until I noticed her almost shy and expectant look. "Right! I design commercial buildings that are also eco-friendly and sustainable." I paused when I saw her eyes shine with admiration. Fuck me! Her open adulation wasn't helping my strange fascination with her.

"Oh, that's so cool," she whispered, before biting her lower lip as if to stop more words from coming out.

I nodded and spoke a little about my work. Before the conversation could continue, Aunt Tanya interrupted. "Kids, can we take this conversation to the living room? I can get some coffee."

Coffee? Shit! Time had flown by. "Ahem, my apologies, it's getting late, and I promised Dad I'd be home for the game."

I stood up, ready to help Aunt Tanya clear the table. The one thing my mom had always instilled in me were manners, and I wasn't about to forget it. Least of all now.

"Don't bother with the table, Zain. I'll take care of it." As always, Uncle Neil jumped to help his wife, the love and affection he had for his wife evident. A sour taste developed in my mouth when I noticed Pari watch her parents fondly. Damn! She was a hearts-and-flowers sort of girl.

"Thanks once again for the lovely dinner." I hugged both of them before nodding at Pari.

"Why don't you walk Zain outside, darling?"

I tried not to wince when I saw Tanya practically push Pari towards the living room. Ah, so she was aware already! Matchmaking TinTin had taken over! I wish Aunt Tanya knew how fucked up I truly was. My brows furrowed at the catastrophe that could follow if I treated Pari like any other fling. Even I couldn't go that far.

"Oh... okay, Mama," Pari stuttered before looking at me. Noticing my severe frown, she glanced away and nodded for me to follow her outside.

I walked after her without haste, admiring her curvy form outlined in the dress. Balling my fists, I felt furious when an unexpected urge to touch her, kiss her, and caress her skin erupted from within. My thoughts refused to die down. I wondered if her skin would be as soft as it looked.

Lost in my thoughts, I didn't realize she'd slowed down after nearing my car. I almost crashed into her tiny form, stopping the collision at the last moment. My hands automatically went to her shoulders to steady her.

"Sorry." I apologized for my uncharacteristic clumsiness.

"It's okay. I'm fine." Pari smiled, looking even more angelic, especially when a dimple appeared in her right cheek.

At her pure, guileless smile, I couldn't help myself any longer. My hands traced the dimple, making her gasp. "You feel this too, don't you?" Never one to beat around the bush, I saw no point in denying our instant attraction. She had to feel this insane pull. I've certainly never had such a powerful reaction towards anyone else, and frankly, it was starting to piss me off.

"I don't know what you're talking about."

When Pari frowned and raised confused eyes towards me, it hit me. She'd never felt this way before. She honestly had no clue what I was talking about. "I hope you never do," I muttered to myself with a sigh. "How old are you?"

"Twenty-one... almost."

I nearly winced. Shit! She was all heart, way too young for me. One more reason I should stay the fuck away from this curvy little angel. She was better off without someone like me, who was jaded and grumpy. But looking at her face, I wanted to touch her just this once. I briefly brushed my thumb against her full lower lip before stepping back from her. "See you soon, angel."

I felt ten feet tall when I saw the blush that stained her cheeks. With a hand raised in a wave, I got into my car. As I drove out of her driveway, my eyes were on her in the rearview mirror. *So long, angel!*

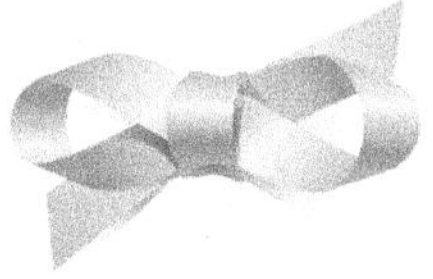

#2

Pari

"**M**om? Can you please send John?" I could practically feel my mom roll her eyes at the other end of the line. But then, I don't blame her. It wasn't the first time I'd made one of my SOS calls. Everyone had their quirks, and mine was directions. Or the lack of it, if I had to be precise.

I had the tendency to get lost in places that are huge and crowded. And malls were both. It wasn't my fault that I was born with this defect. I can walk around in circles despite following exits and signs. It's an art, to be honest!

"Again? I thought we gave you enough pointers, sweetie."

I heard my mom's voice and came out of my thoughts. Yes, the same pointers that I'd abandoned ten minutes prior. Before I could reply, I heard my mom sigh over the phone. "It didn't work, did it? Honey, next time, don't go alone and scare the living daylights out of me or daddy. Your dad doesn't know I sent you alone. He'd throw a fit if he knew."

"All right," I mumbled, while wishing the earth would swallow me up. I was almost twenty-one, for God's sake. Thanks to my parents' wealth and my dad's paranoia, I rarely did things alone, but this had to stop. I didn't want to be treated like a child anymore. That's why I'd begged Mom to let me go alone to a nearby mall that wasn't too far from my place.

Usually, John, my chauffeur and security, who'd accompanied ever since I was ten, stayed with me. This time, however, I wanted to go by myself, prove to myself I could be a responsible adult. Ignoring the little voice inside me that questioned the timing of this urge, I listened to Mom's voice on the other end.

"Where exactly are you inside the mall? Do you see any cafes where you can wait? John is on an errand, but I'm calling him right away. Stay where it's safe."

"Yes, Mama." I gave her the name of a popular coffee shop before making a beeline towards it. Once in, I wanted to order a coffee to go and stood in line. Ten minutes later, with a cold brew in hand, I turned around only to bump into a familiar figure. "Oh, I'm so sorry!" I apologized in a breathless voice.

My eyes widened seeing Zain standing before me, his gray eyes staring into mine with laser focus. Did I just conjure him up from my thoughts? I wouldn't be entirely surprised if that happened. Because he'd constantly been in my thoughts the past few days. Ever since that dinner.

I'd had dreams of him, and he'd done some pretty hot things to me in my dreams. Something that had never happened before. Not even with my favorite book boyfriends. I froze, hoping my thoughts weren't visible in my face. My breath hitched lightly when his eyes traced my face and lips. I sipped my coffee hurriedly, hoping to hide my nervousness and desire behind the cup.

"Fancy seeing you here. Shopping?" I pretended I wasn't lost, and it was a normal occurrence for me to get a coffee on the go. I waited for the perfect opportunity to move away after a friendly greeting, but to my dismay Zain tangled my fingers in his and pulled me out of the cafe.

"Zain!" I hissed and looked around, hoping no one noticed the tall man who was pulling me out of the crowd. "Zain, wait! Where are you taking me?" To my chagrin, he continued to pull me farther down a path where the exit appeared magically.

"Hold on! I'm waiting for someone."

I saw him frown before he slowed down. "Who?" he grunted.

"How does that concern you?" My nose twitched in anger. The nerve of this arrogant, hot, yummy-looking... I mean, arrogant man.

"Who?" he asked me again, scowling at the prospect of me meeting someone in the mall.

"John." I sighed.

Zain grunted and continued to walk until we reached his SUV.

"Wait! Why are you kidnapping me? Are you kidnapping me? I don't know if I'm supposed to continue walking with you." I threw the last bit at him in sheer exasperation.

Instead of replying, I heard him chuckle. Annoyed, I followed him with a huff. Wait till I raise a ruckus. I could totally do that! Maybe after I finished admiring his perfect ass, I told myself. Whatever! Humph!!!

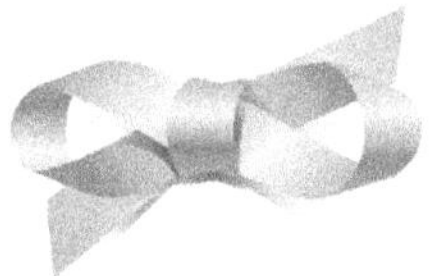

Zain

The moment I made my sexy little angel sit inside my car, I heaved a sigh of relief. She was safe and within my sight. I prayed she wouldn't scream or create a scene in the mall. Not that she was a match against my strength. Still, I hated any form of violence, especially against women and children. And my angel was even more precious than most.

When I sensed the glare directed at me, I couldn't help it. I chuckled, my face immediately morphing into surprise. In the last half hour, I'd almost laughed… twice! It felt strange; I don't remember the last time I felt… happy. "Relax, angel, your mom sent me to pick you up."

"What?" The speed with which her face morphed from annoyance to dismay was almost comical.

"Yeah." I reversed out of the parking spot and put the car in motion.

"Why would she do that? What did she tell you?" Her frown was adorable and so was the blush that crept up her face. I looked at her sideways as she continued to glare and mutter to herself, a trait that was all too endearing.

"That you were lost." My voice was deceptively mild. I wanted to spank Pari's adorable bottom for venturing out alone and getting lost.

"Yes, I was." I saw her accept she'd been lost with an embarrassed frown.

"How does someone get lost in a mall where there are floor maps and exit signs?" I didn't realize I'd spoken out loud, not until Pari shrank into herself. I almost cursed myself for thinking aloud when I felt her go all quiet on me.

After a few minutes, I stopped the car in front of her house. Before she could open the door and slip out, I caught her wrist. "Hey, I didn't mean to be judgmental or rude. It was a genuine question. I was just curious."

Her dark gaze zoomed into mine, as if to check if I was being honest. A few seconds later, satisfied, her expression cleared. She sighed before speaking softly. "Well, it baffles me, too, but it has already happened so many times that Dad is scared to let me out alone. After his recent popularity as this cool techie guy, my family doesn't want to take any chances. They're not entirely sure what I'd do or where I'd end up, you know?"

As though all this didn't bother her, Pari shrugged; her t-shirt moved, exposing one creamy shoulder. All my thoughts skidded to a halt as my vision zeroed in on her creamy skin. Without thinking, I trailed the back of my hand over the exposed skin before pulling the fabric in place.

Pari gasped and shifted back as if she'd been burned. I saw her visibly swallow, her eyes clouding with desire and confusion.

Mine, my inner voice growled, terrifying me. This possessiveness was new. A slight tremor hit my hand as I gripped the steering wheel. From the corner of my eyes, I saw Pari's mouth open and close before she gave up and leaned back. Good! I wasn't sure I was in any position to answer any of her questions right now. If only I knew the answers myself.

"I think I should leave now," Pari whispered, although it seemed like she was asking my permission.

I felt my dick lengthen against my slacks. Was she asking for my permission? Would she always ask my permission for everything if we ever gave into our attraction? Would she wait for me to give her the permission to come? I blinked, surprised at my wayward thoughts. I wasn't even sure I was ready for a relationship. Yet here I was, thinking about controlling her orgasms. Fuck!

Stumped, I refrained from saying anything. Instead, I waited, wanting to see what she'd do next. I expected a shy smile or a thank you, but nothing would have prepared me for the words that came out of her sinful mouth.

"I haven't been kissed. Ever," she whispered with curious eyes that subtly moved to my lips before coming back to my eyes. As soon as the words left her mouth, she gasped, as if only then realizing what she'd unwittingly revealed. Before she could open the door and bolt out, I caught her arm.

"Be careful about what you wish for, angel. You're probably not ready for a man like me. I don't do relationships. A good fuck is all I can provide." I paused when I felt her eyes widen in shock.

My stare captured her big, beautiful eyes. I've been told I could make a person cower away with my cold, unblinking stare. For my angel's sake, I hoped I succeeded. I cared about Uncle Neil and Aunt Tanya. For all our sakes, I hoped I didn't end up hurting this innocent beauty who was looking at me with her fuck-me eyes.

"I think you're lying to yourself and me, pretending only I want... kisses... and other things. I want to be kissed." She spoke in a low, soft tone. "By you," she added, just before she bolted out of her seat.

Shocked, I looked on as she practically ran from the SUV. Leaning back in my seat, I pinched the bridge of my nose and willed my body to calm down. I'd been deliberately crude, wanting to push her away. I didn't expect her honesty. It was... unsettling. No games or pretense; she conveyed her needs clearly, making me rock hard. The minx! She'd turned the tables smoothly. Motherfucking hell!

Exhaling forcefully, I put the vehicle in motion and drove to my parents' place, where I was staying until my place was ready to move in.

As I drove up to my parents' mansion, I tried to my best not to think of Pari. And failed. Visions of taking her in the filthiest ways possible were already filling my soul. It didn't occur to me, not even then, that for a man who wasn't into commitment or relationships, I was fast approaching a head-on collision.

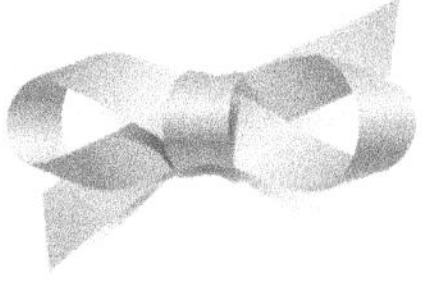

#3

Zain

A Few Weeks Later

I let myself into my parents' mansion using my key, pausing when I heard a soft giggle. Pocketing my key, I walked through the huge, tastefully done living room to the kitchen. My frozen heart thawed when I saw my mom and Pari cooking something on the stove. They were whispering among themselves and giggling before continuing to add something into the pan.

I stared at the beautiful sight in front of me, basking in the perfection in the room. Pari was dressed in a bright blue dress that molded to her generous curves. She seemed to radiate happiness and cheer, totally at ease with my mom and the surroundings. I'd missed her. Which was weird because we weren't best friends or anything. Yet there was a flutter in my heart when I looked at her. Willing my body not to react at the sight of Pari, I cleared my throat before I spoke. "Mom?"

The two of them turned around and I could practically see my angel startle and blush even from this distance.

"Oh, hey, honey. Welcome home. Pari and I were just fixing dinner for all of us."

As always, when I saw my mom, my heart constricted and something pierced deep into that organ. She was the sweetest soul on this earth and one of the primary reasons I'm alive. Despite being a famous pastry chef, she was one of the most simple and humble souls I've come across in my life. And now, seeing her with my angel made me warm in places that were previously frozen and sealed.

I swallowed my fear when I realized how easily Pari could get under my skin. From experience I knew such deep feelings wouldn't end well for me.

"Did you have a busy day?" my mom inquired, interrupting my thoughts. With practice, I schooled my face not to reveal my inner thoughts, glad my mom's cheerful voice broke my overthinking.

"Yes, Mom. We completed most of the details for the first site that Dad was talking about."

My mom beamed at me, her eyes shining with pride and love. All for me. Even after all these years, every time I received her unconditional love, I was humbled. I doubt even my birth mother would have been this supportive. As my dad always liked to say, Mia was the heart of the Malik household and I completely agreed.

I didn't show any of my thoughts to her. I couldn't; not even if I tried. "I'll freshen up and come down, Mom." I nodded at Pari before taking two stairs at a time.

Barely a minute later, I heard a knock at my door. Unbuttoning my shirt, I simultaneously walked to the door and pulled it open. To my surprise, there was my curvy angel, standing with my phone in her hand. "You le-left this on the kitchen island. You received a call."

Her eyes seemed to widen endlessly when she took in my state of partial undress. I wasn't even going to think about that adorable stutter. I raised a brow, finding her rapt stare equally amusing and arousing. Instead of taking the phone from her hand, I grabbed her by the wrist and pulled her into my room.

I caught my angel just as she stumbled and almost lost her balance. "Easy," I murmured into her ear, almost smiling, when I heard a tiny gasp escape her mouth. Ignoring the urge to pull her closer, I held her away from my body, absently noticing she barely reached my chin.

"Ugh, stop pulling me wherever you feel like. You seem to do it way too often."

She stared at me, her face displaying her exasperation and the desire she couldn't hide. Trying hard not to ogle my chest and failing, she wiggled away from my hold to walk around the enormous room.

I stood back and watched her move around my space just as a butterfly would move in a garden. When my eyes moved down the dress that barely reached her knees, my blood began pounding in my ears. With her loose hair, curious eyes, and shining light, she was an obsession I couldn't get rid of.

The past few weeks, I'd fantasized about her, corrupting her in the filthiest ways. Exhaling, I adjusted my pants discreetly, knowing she was the one thing I couldn't have.

"Ooh, these are so beautiful. How come we don't have any photos together? All the photos that I have are with Aarav," she asked aloud, frowning at the few family photos that my mom had snapped without my knowledge.

Aarav was my younger brother and my parents' biological child. Hearing her ponder about the lack of memories of me with the extended family, my thoughts turned dark. I'd come into this family when I'd turned twelve, and even then, it had taken me a long time to process all the shit that had happened in my formative years.

I hadn't been close to anyone apart from my mom and dad. Vaguely, I recalled a young Pari running around with her ponytails. When Pari turned around, I was lost in my thoughts, for once not registering her beautiful face.

"Do you... you know, have any contact with your... biological family?" Pari asked me hesitatingly, curiosity brimming in her dark eyes.

I shook my head no. My thoughts turned dark with remembered pain. Unaware of my inner turmoil, she asked me the dreaded question. "If you don't mind me asking, what happened?"

I saw her walk towards me and felt the familiar constriction close around my throat. The feeling of claustrophobia and helplessness threatened to consume me. I hated talking about my biological family. Even if it was Pari who was asking me the question.

"I understand if you don't want to..."

"No!"

"I'm sorry..."

"This is not up for discussion," I snapped, making her jump in nervousness. I breathed in and out, focusing on my breathing. Feeling the familiar anxiety creep up at the thought of my biological family, I tried to breathe and focus. Forcing down the bile rising up my throat, I picked up the towel lying on my bed and walked into the bathroom, slamming the door in my frustration.

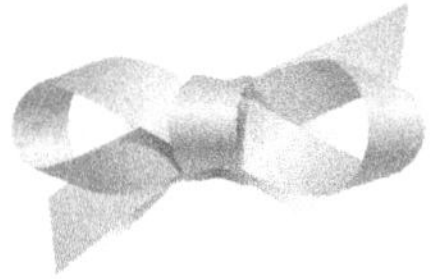

Pari

I watched Zain walk away from me with trembling lips. My eyes brimmed when I realized he was probably done with me. I'd done it again; I'd let my mouth run away. A trait that rarely bothered my family. Well, they were family, and they loved me despite my quirks. The rest of the world didn't have similar obligations.

But I had no intention of hurting Zain. My skin prickled with awareness every time I was in his vicinity. My body absorbed his energy, sensing his pain. I couldn't help but ask, wanting to make him feel better.

As an empath, I tended to avoid distressing or overwhelming people. But with Zain, somehow, I couldn't do it. Thanks to my ability to feel things so deeply, I couldn't ever play games or pretend I don't feel certain emotions. I preferred honesty with myself and others. Clearly, that wasn't acceptable. Not with Zain.

Wiping away the few tears that had escaped from my eyes, I sniffled before leaving the room quietly.

After composing myself, I walked down and stepped into the kitchen to see Uncle Armaan hugging Aunt Mia. They looked adorable together, and Mia was secretly my favorite among all my aunts. Although, I suppose I couldn't really choose if someone asked.

"Darling, I didn't know you were here. No wonder my home is brighter today." Uncle Armaan declared in his usual flamboyant style before he enveloped me in a tight hug.

I smiled when I felt him kiss my temple. I loved this man who had a heart of gold. "Hello, Uncle Armaan. I was here to help Aunt Mia with some stuff, and it had been a while since I came over, you know."

"I agree. If it were up to me, you'll live with us. Neil could go get himself another daughter."

I heard Mia giggle behind me and grinned. "It might be a little too late for that, don't you think? Anyway, I'm so sorry, but I gotta rush. Kiara is in town and she's coming home. I can't stay for dinner." Kiara was my BFF, and we'd been thick since childhood.

"Oh! Aarav was so looking forward to seeing you." Mia's soft voice was filled with genuine regret.

"I'm sorry, Aunt Mia. I'll be back soon. I promise," I assured Aunt Mia before giving her a tight hug. "Bye!"

Five minutes later, I was in my car, driving back to my place. Exhaling once the house was behind me, I sent a silent prayer. Thank God, I'd left before the two of them sensed I was upset. I didn't want to stay for a meal with Zain seated across from me. I'd never have been able to pretend all was well. Blinking away my tears, I drove on, for once not enjoying the view or the drive.

. . ❧ . .

HOURS LATER, I WAS lying on my bed, going over the same words for the tenth time. After I'd come home, I hadn't bothered with dinner or socializing with my family. Instead, I locked myself in my room, my heart heavy.

I tried a lavender bath, and it didn't work. Spending time with my book boyfriends? That didn't work either. Which was something, since reading always put me in a good mood. Sighing, I abandoned my book when I heard a rap on my window. I ignored the sound, blaming it on the wind. Lounging in my pajama shorts and camisole, I was in no mood to get out of my bed.

Thinking about Zain and how he'd walked away brought me a fresh bout of pain. I didn't understand my powerful reaction to him. Was it because he was Mia and Armaan's son? Or was it because he was the only guy I've liked *that way* so far? The questions were whirling around in my mind, not letting me lie down in peace.

Confused and frustrated, I once again tried to get back to the book I'd been reading when I heard the noise again. This time, I knew I couldn't ignore the sound. Turning towards the window, I gasped when I saw the shadow of a person on the other side. Quickly searching for a weapon and finding none, I settled for the paperback of an alien romance I'd been reading. Well, at least it was something, I told myself. Moving stealthily, I opened the French window and raised my hand that held the book.

Before I could attack or scream, I was pushed inside, and a male hand caught my wrist. My book fell with a thud. At that instant, I realized it was Zain, and he'd once again tugged me into a room.

"What the hell! Zain, you scared the living hell out of me! What are you doing here?" I hissed, glaring at him for good measure. Knowing my parents were on the same floor, I couldn't raise my voice. I doubted they'd appreciate Zain sneaking into my room at this hour, anyway.

"I wanted to talk to you."

Zain shrugged before he bent down to pick up my book. When he smirked, I knew he'd guessed it was no ordinary fantasy. What can I say? I enjoyed reading steamy romance novels that also included horns and tails! That didn't mean I cared about his opinion. Or anyone else's about my reading choices.

"And you can stop smirking." I snatched the book out of his hand before placing it on the table with a thud.

"I wasn't trying to judge your reading material." His smile widened when I growled. "I was more amused at your choice of weapon. Did you honestly think you could hurt me with that?" He raised a brow.

I narrowed my eyes. "It's none of your business. Anyway, what on earth made you sneak in here like this? There's a front door that works perfectly well."

"You left."

His accusatory tone got to me. *What!? Was he even real?* "Yeah, well, you yelled and walked away from me first, remember?" I glared at him for good measure.

"I'm sorry."

My eyes widened at his quiet apology. I didn't expect him to apologize, but something in his tone made my eyes prickle. Sniffling, I bit back a retort. I hated fights and loved to be happy. But this man was constantly titling my world, making me feel things I wasn't used to. It scared me, honestly.

"Angel, please don't cry."

He pulled me into his arms, engulfing me in his warmth. For a moment, I allowed myself to enjoy the spicy scent that was uniquely Zain. I felt his steely muscles beneath the soft fabric of his shirt. Hmm, I could stay like this forever. My eyes snapped open, reminding me I owed him an apology.

"I'm sorry, too, for crossing a boundary, but that didn't mean you could yell at me or walk away from me like that. For what it's worth, I was trying to backtrack and apologize when you cut me off rudely. I didn't know whether I should stay and try to talk to you, or if you were done..." I paused. How could I assume there was something between us in the first place? We weren't... anything... really.

I felt him place gentle fingers beneath my chin. "Angel, I'm sorry. I don't like to talk about my past. It always gets to me." He sighed. "Believe me, it wasn't intentional."

I remained mum, trying to hide my pain and how hurt I was by his action.

"Hey, I said I'm sorry." He caught my chin, gently forcing me to look at him.

"Okay!" Only then did I realize I was still in his arms. I stared at him, noticing his muscular forearms that held me and the small patch of his tanned skin that peeked from his shirt. Realizing any moment my body could betray me, I wriggled out of his hold. "Ugh! Why am I in your arms?"

"For..." he murmured, his gray eyes darkening.

"For what?" I whispered, my mouth going dry at his look.

"This."

He bent down to kiss me, his lips gently moving over mine. The touch of his lips reminded me of the first rays of sunshine and the gentle flutter of a butterfly wing all rolled into one. I went on my toes to move into him, only to be lifted by him as if I weighed nothing. He carried me to my bed, all while his lips gently coaxed mine apart.

Instinctively, I knew he wanted me to follow his lead, and I moved my lips against his. My fingers ran over his arms, thrilled to feel his muscles bunch beneath my touch. Groaning, he slid his tongue against mine, deepening the kiss, just as he laid me down on my bed.

I felt the soft mattress behind me before the delicious, unfamiliar weight of Zain pressed on top of me. Thrilling at the contact with his solid heat, I caught his shirt, trying to pull him closer. Oh, this was so sexy, hot, and completely surreal.

Zain grunted and bit me, tugging at my lower lip with his teeth. "Breathe," I heard the amusement in his tone and realized I was holding on to my breath. He moved back a little, his eyes staring into mine. "Your first kiss," he murmured softly, caressing my lower lip with his thumb.

My first kiss, just the way I wanted. I gulped. My lips tingled and my breathing was all over the place. I didn't realize my hands were holding on to his shirt, nor did it enter my mind that I was writhing beneath him suggestively, not until I heard him groan.

"Pari, stop moving, baby. I'm a red-blooded man, not a saint. Before I lose my head completely, let me get out. I wanted to make sure we were okay." He tilted his head slightly, capturing my eyes and my heart. "Are we good?"

I looked at Zain, realizing this was the most he'd spoken to me in all the times we'd been together. "Guess so," I absently murmured. When I felt him kiss me softly once more, I knew it was too late. I was already beginning to fall for this grumpy man. My treacherous body had taken over my pragmatic mind. Even the imminent risk of a heartbreak didn't stop my heart from fluttering.

I watched him tear himself away from me with a dazed expression. "Goodnight, my angel. Sleep tight." When he adjusted himself, I felt a fiery blush stain my cheeks. Hurriedly, I averted my eyes away from him, silently groaning when I sensed him smile at my self-consciousness.

Long after Zain let himself out, I stayed on my bed, in the same position, staring at the ceiling. Searching for answers. My first kiss, and it exceeded all my expectations. No fiction could ever compare to Zain's lips and touches. Sighing, I rolled over with a soft groan, pressing my face into the pillow. My senses were on overload after my first kiss, making my head buzz.

The next morning, after the adrenaline had come down, I felt reality seeping in. I realized the danger I was in with Zain. Unlike the fairytale endings that existed in my books, the looming reality of a heartbreak rang like warning bells in my head. Blazing chemistry aside, would my heart survive a relationship with Zain?

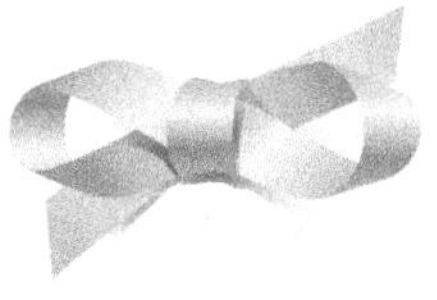

#4

Pari

"This is one of the best cheesecakes I've ever tasted."

I smiled at Uncle Arjun, my favorite among my dad's three best friends. I still hear stories about how I had a special affinity towards Uncle Arjun ever since I was born. Well, it's hard not to love the gruff but soft ex-army man. "Thanks, Uncle A. I love cooking for you."

I saw him place his fork on his plate and lean back. He smiled lightly, but his eyes remained serious. "Now that we're done with your delicious cheesecake, I wanted to talk to you about something."

"That sounds serious." I sat down next to him, taking a fork to dig into my plate.

"I don't know if it is. You need to tell me."

I looked up from the plate. "What?"

"Why did Zain enter your room last night? Especially through the window? Stealthily, I presume?"

"Uncle A!" I gasped, my face flushing with embarrassment. Trust him to monitor every little thing. After all, he owned a security company and ensured our property remained safe. "That's... he... uh..." I trailed off, unsure how much he knew and how much I'd have to tell him. What could I say, anyway? That Zain was into me? We were dating? Honestly, I didn't know. It was only one kiss. A yummy, toe-curling one at that, but yeah! I surely couldn't ask Zain to marry me after one kiss, right?

"Sweetheart, right now, I'm not pounding my first into his jaw only because he is Armaan's son. But if anyone messes with my girl, they might as well be dead." The last part was a growl.

"Uncle A!" I hissed. "Okay, first, you gotta stop speaking about killing people. And don't you dare tattle to Mom and Dad. Please," I pleaded to my godfather, who thought the world revolved around me. Sweet, but lethal. Especially during situations like these.

Arjun sighed. "Fine. But promise me you'll be careful. You call me if someone ever dares to cross the line with you. Got it?"

"Yes, yes, of course!" I frantically nodded. "I've never given you any reason to kill anyone in the past. Umm... I truly like Zain and I want to... I want to see where this is going." This time, I ensured I fixed my irresistible pout and puppy dog eyes in place.

Arjun smiled, seeing through my antics. Thank God! I was off the hook. For now! Growing up, my mom had thrown quite a lot of hissy fits when Uncle A spoiled me rotten against her wishes. But it had been fun. I literally was the apple of everyone's eyes since I was the first "baby" in their group, and I couldn't be more grateful for this wonderful extended family.

"If your mom knew I'm aware of this, she'd kill me for hiding your secret. You know that, right?" Arjun raised a brow.

I giggled. "I can imagine. But then you know her, Uncle A. She loves to play matchmaker." I paused when I saw him frown. "What? What did I say wrong?"

He sighed. "Nothing! I hate the fact that you're growing up too fast and men can be assh..." He broke off, shaking his head in defeat.

Placing my fork on my plate, I caught Uncle Arjun's hand. "I promise I'll be careful, okay? And if Zain makes me cry, you can punch him. Deal?"

Arjun simply pulled me in for a hug and kissed my temple lightly. "It'll be more than a punch. Take care, darling. Be safe."

"I promise," I whispered.

. . ⚜ . .

I SHUT MY BOOK WITH a force that surprised even me. Seven days! It had been seven days and three hours since Zain had broken into my room and stolen my first kiss. Being new to the whole guys and relationships thing, I didn't know if it was okay to call him or text him. I didn't want to seem desperate by making the first move. Especially after my unintentional prodding at his parents' place the last time.

Despite my apprehension, I casually inquired about him when I'd spoken to Aunt Mia two days ago. I hoped she'd tell him I asked about him. Still nothing! Even after all the waiting and twisted efforts, nothing. Ugh! Coming to a quick decision, I sat up from my couch. I wasn't my mother's daughter if I didn't do something about this. Did he think I'd pine for him? Fat chance!

I remembered the conversation I had with my best friend, Kiara, the previous day. After her master's, she was back at her parents' place, applying for internships and entry-level positions. When she'd seen me incessantly check my phone for messages, she suggested I try dating other men just to get out of my funk. It didn't sound appealing then, but now I was desperate to try something, anything, to get Zain out of my head.

Snatching my phone from my desk, I downloaded a dating app and uploaded a pic of mine. I keyed in some information about myself and sat back, satisfied. Just because I signed up didn't mean I was about to hook up with random men. But I didn't need to tell anyone that, right?

Hoping to gain some footing in the dating game, I hoped I could casually go out on a date or two to know how things worked. Unfortunately, none of my romance books taught me how real-life dating worked. In my books, it all was magical. The couple seemed to fall in love instantly and they seemed to know he or she was *the one* within seconds of meeting them. I only wish it were that easy in real life.

In my case, in all honesty, it had exactly been like those books. Bam, and it hit me. It was as if the universe had brought Zain to me out of nowhere with neon signs. Why wasn't he declaring his love then?

For a moment, my mind wandered to that epic kiss I'd already relived a zillion times. I haven't slept properly the entire seven days, the memory of his touch invading my sleep. I'd been awoken by erotic dreams that involved a shirtless Zain and his very talented mouth. Feeling my nipples tauten underneath my top, I cursed under my breath.

Zain was the reason for the frustrating, unresolved sexual needs in me. He better fix them or else... With a soft groan, I got up to take a shower and log in to my classes. Time for action. No more waiting around!

Zain

"**S**o, this is where you love to spend your time, eh?" I looked around the huge library before addressing my angel, who was studiously ignoring me. Or rather, trying to. My lips tilted slightly when I heard her mutter something to herself. Cute!

After our kiss, I'd been shaken to my core. I'd stayed away from Pari, not wanting to lead her on or break her heart. Although the memory of that kiss ruined me in the best way possible, I'd tried my darndest to stay away. But fate had other ideas.

I'd received a restoration request for this library that was built during the British colonization period. The carved staircases, huge ceilings, and the beautiful windows spoke of the architecture during that time. I'd grabbed the project, knowing it wasn't like the usual high value commercial projects that I worked on. This was more passion than business. As I looked around, inspecting, taking it all in, my eyes spotted a figure I'd recognize anywhere.

Immediately, my legs started moving towards Pari, who was picking out a book from one of the shelves. The minute my eyes landed on my angel, I felt my heart constrict with an unknown feeling. It was... strange, even disturbing. Looking at the way Pari pursed her lips, my mind jolted back to the kiss.

I mean, holy fuck, it was one of the best kisses of my life. I wasn't a saint, not by anyone's standards, and I've been with enough women in my life to know this was special.

The memory of that kiss derailed me in a way that I didn't expect. I'd jacked off to the memory of Pari on her bed, her silky hair spread on her pillow, looking like sin and seduction. I should have been embarrassed by the sheer number of times I'd gotten myself off. Not even in my teens had my body been this excited. Given her eagerness, I knew it wouldn't take me much to seduce her, but I couldn't afford to do it. Not with our family dynamics.

Work, too, was killing me. A lot was riding on the timeline for my project, and it was already hell dealing with bureaucracy. One would think the system would make it easier to design and get the approvals for sustainable buildings that focused on energy conservation, but reality was very different.

It had been frustrating to work with the officials to get the required approvals and sign-offs. Despite my last name and my father's influence, I could only get so far.

I exhaled, coming back to the present to see my angel trying to eye me surreptitiously. I hid the beginnings of a smile and continued to look at her. She was anything but sneaky, and I knew she couldn't hold a grudge to save her life.

After our kiss, I'd gone back to my parents' place and asked Aarav about Pari. What I didn't expect was for him to come to me with memories, stories, and photos. He didn't ask me why I wanted to know about Pari. Instead, he'd shared all the sweet memories of my angel. The more I saw Pari's face through her growing-up years and read all the birthday and congratulatory cards she'd written for Aarav, the more I craved her.

I thought I'd successfully suppressed my needs. That was until I spotted her in the library, amidst the books, her ass enclosed in denim shorts and a t-shirt that read 'I love book boyfriends.' Of course she did!

"What are you doing here?"

I heard her whisper-yell and coughed to suppress my laugh. "What? Am I not allowed to be in this library?"

"Very funny! Next, you'll tell me you like to read romance." She rolled her eyes at me. The minx.

"Careful, if you did that when we're alone, I'd spank you," I murmured into her ear softly.

I felt her stiffen before her eyes widened comically. Her crimson face turned towards me before she huffed out a breath. "You are unbelievable."

"Because I want to spank you? Don't you love it when the women in your books get spanked?"

"Because you've got some nerve to come and bullshit me after a week of silence," she snapped. She pursed her lips when a few readers looked up. "What the duck!" I heard her mutter to herself before she gathered her things. I was so lost in her beauty that I didn't realize she was walking away from me. With a muttered curse, I stumbled behind her in haste.

I followed my angel out of the library not so sneakily, catching up with her outside the library.

"What the duck?" I chuckled at her curse, belatedly noticing her trying to move away from me.

Hearing my amused sound, she glared at me. "That's how Mom used to curse when we were kids and it... it stuck. Okay?"

My smile widened at her explanation. She was so darn cute! "Truce?" I walked a few steps ahead and turned to face her.

"Stop! Before you go any farther, this isn't how it works with me. You just can't... can't walk away and step back in whenever you feel like it. It's all so frigging confusing."

My smile vanished when I heard the distress in her voice. "Angel, I'm sorry." I moved a step forward, only for her to step back.

"Zain, I'll be honest with you. I don't know what I'm doing, okay? I've never felt like this before, and I am clearly out of my depth. My inexperience is definitely not helping my case. The kiss was so... uh, it was everything I wanted in a first kiss and more. But that doesn't give you the right to ghost me." She rushed on before I could interrupt. "So, yeah, I signed up on a dating app and I have a date this evening. I want to know how this... this whole dating thing works."

My blood chilled in my veins. "Motherfucking hell!" I snarled and stopped when I saw her flinch. "What do you mean, you have a date? Seriously?" I was barely holding on to my control. Was she out of her damn mind?

When I saw her lips tremble, I visibly calmed. Rather, I tried to. "Pari, don't act in haste," I pleaded. I saw red at the prospect of another man even looking at Pari. I sure as hell couldn't handle the thought of her going out with random assholes who'll take advantage of her sweetness.

But I had to tread carefully. My angel was soft and skittish, and she was one of the gentlest souls I've met. I had to rein in my possessiveness and jealousy. At least until I figured what was going on with me.

She shook her head. "No, I have to do this. Anyway, it's too late to cancel now. The date is in two hours. I need to go home and get ready."

Making a split-second decision, I caught her wrist. "I'll drop you off at home. Where's your date?"

"Oh, no! That's none of your business. I'm not telling you anything about this date."

I pinched the bridge of my nose, praying for some patience. "Fine. I'll take you home. At least give me that. Please."

"Alright."

She shrugged and walked ahead, her denim-clad ass testing my control. Trying not to ogle and failing, I followed her like a puppy, all the while wondering how I could gain more information about her fucking date. How could I kill the man without evidence?

As I moved towards my car, I tried not to listen to the voice that told me this looked a lot like commitment. Which would invariably lead to heartbreak. Was I ready to face yet another failure in relationships? Ignoring the sudden heaviness in my chest, I opened the door for Pari before slipping into the driver's seat. After texting my contact inside the library about an emergency, I placed the device in the console and started the car.

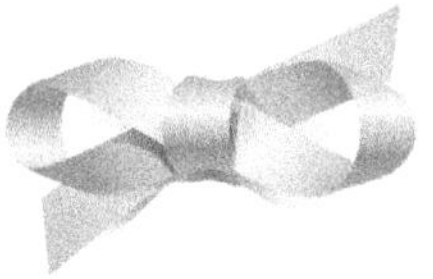

#5

Pari

I spritzed some perfume on my wrists and behind my ears before looking at myself one last time in the mirror. Here I was, ready for my date. My black skirt and crop top looked stylish enough for an upscale restaurant. Which is where I was meeting my date. But thanks to one pesky, handsome pain in the grass (Oh yeah, another one of my mom's alternative cuss words that stuck with me), my heart wasn't in it.

I clicked my tongue impatiently before picking up my sling bag. Time to enjoy the evening! As I walked down the stairs, I could hear my parents talking. My mother noticed me all dressed up and paused.

"Darling, where are you off to? You'll be back on time, right?" Hearing her tone, I knew it wasn't really a question.

"Mom..."

"Don't *Mom* me. You know the rules."

"I agree with your mom, sweetheart. Now, where are you off to?" My dad snaked his arm around my mom's waist and looked at me.

"On a date." I bit my lip, hating myself for sounding hesitant. I saw my mom's brows go up, but wisely, she said nothing. Unfortunately, I couldn't say the same thing about my dad.

"Date? Who are you going out with? Do we know him? How do you know he's not a serial killer or a rapist?"

"Daddy!" I was horrified to realize I was genuinely scared. Never did I consider these possibilities when I decided to meet a stranger. But then again, that's how these stupid dating apps worked! All I had was a username and, hopefully, an actual picture of the guy.

"You're not driving. John will stay and drop you back at home safely," my dad declared, his eyes turning steely.

"Neil, you're getting worked up and stressing our little girl. We'll track her location and she'll have us on speed dial. John will call us if they have any issues. Right?"

I exhaled and threw a grateful look at my mom. On those rare occasions when my dad turned all alpha and stubborn, my usually hot mess of a mom calmed him down and turned rational. They were a weird pair who were still very much in love.

They fell in love while my dad attempted to teach her to date and flirt. I couldn't believe my parents would do something that wild. Yet, every time I heard how they met and fell for each other, it was like listening to a fairy tale all over. I sighed! My parents were the reason I was single with zero experience. I wanted what they had, and I thought I might have found that. Until Zain...

Cutting off my thoughts about him, I cleared my throat before speaking. "Dad, I promise I'll turn on my mobile location and keep it on."

"I'm still not convinced. Maybe you shouldn't date until you're thirty," he growled, a severe frown etching his handsome face.

"Daddy!" I admonished him softly before throwing an exasperated glance at him. "Mom had me when she was in her mid-twenties." I grinned when I heard my mom giggle.

My dad glared at both of us before making me promise that I'd be careful. He reluctantly let me go, but not before clarifying that he hated boys. Especially the ones who looked at his little girl.

Waving them goodbye, I walked toward the foyer. I checked my appearance one last time with my hand mirror, my parents' conversation muffled from this distance.

"You know she cannot meet strangers!" I could hear my dad's frustration. He didn't want me to be ensnared by any asshole, and all boys were assholes for his little girl. I got it.

"She won't!" I heard Mom reassure him. Grateful for their love despite their overprotective tendencies, I paused to check if I had my ID, phone, wallet, and all the essentials. Meanwhile, their conversation had continued, although I couldn't catch the complete drift.

"What? How? Don't you dare come up with your crazy schemes now..." There was a brief silence before I heard Dad's voice. "Who are you calling?"

I walked on toward the car, not catching my mom's reply.

"Well, you're going to help me keep my mind off negative thoughts for a couple of hours."

Ouch, my dad's growly tone and my mom's flirty giggle meant... Gross! I couldn't wait to get into the waiting car, not wanting to think about my parents doing the deed.

. . ⁓ . .

THE MINUTE I ENTERED the upscale restaurant PLUS BAR (dumb me, I didn't bother to check that and nor did my date mention it); I knew it wasn't my sort of place. This place had opened fairly recently, and the music was too loud for my preference. It also seemed to be way too crowded. To think that I'd explicitly mentioned I didn't do crowds in my bio. Clearly, my date didn't care about my preferences.

I tried not to bolt, but things only seemed to get worse. To my dismay, we were now seated on barstools. Both me and my date, Pete, who didn't have any qualms about having some appetizers and a beer.

Pete was fairly easy on the eyes, and one could even say he was cute in a boyish sort of way. I shut off the thoughts that threatened to conjure up the image of another man. *Shhh, not now,* I shushed that voice.

"Umm, I'm not old enough to drink. I'll be twenty-one in a couple of months. Sorry!"

"Oh! Okay. Can I get you juice or something?"

Every passing minute, it was more and more evident that he hadn't thought about this whole thing fully. Or maybe the whole app experience wasn't about dating. Perhaps online dating was a euphemism for hookups. As usual, the minute these thoughts and doubts arose in my mind, I began to overthink. My mom had always warned me that my overactive mind would get me into trouble. Looks like that was about to happen starting now.

"So, hmm, I went through your profile, of course, and I stalked you on Insta as well."

I tried not to react when I heard the word 'stalk'. Was he a serial killer? I waited for him to continue. I imagined he'd talk about my pics, but to my surprise, what my date spouted was far worse.

"You're Neil Grover's daughter, right? It's so cool, dude. What is it like living with him?"

I tried not to groan out loud. Not again! In the past, I've had more than a few tech enthusiasts ask me pertinent questions about my dad. Yes, he was this amazing tech billionaire guy who had quite a few tech inventions under his belt, and he was handsome. But hey, underneath all that, he was a person with feelings.

It was worse with women. They called him 'Daddy' right to my face. Eww! It was my dad, for pity's sake. Ugh!!! I tried not to shudder and took a halting breath. Before I could steer the conversation to a generic topic, I saw a familiar figure slide onto the stool next to Pete.

What the actual... It was the bane of my existence, Zain, who seemed to stalk me endlessly. Didn't he have a job or something? How on earth did he know about the location of my date? I refused to believe this was a coincidence. When I noticed Pete check an incoming message, I discreetly glared at Zain. He simply raised a brow at me before ordering whiskey and water for himself.

Whatever! I wasn't going to even think about Zain. He could sit here all he liked. With that thought, I completely ignored Zain and concentrated on Pete. It had been twenty minutes since we'd arrived, and we were still sitting on the barstools. "Let's not talk about my dad. Being on a date and all that." I smiled brightly, trying to move on from the topic.

Despite addressing Pete, my eyes somehow seemed to notice the black shirt that clung to Zain's muscles. I didn't dare look at the jeans. Or the way they stretched over his... *Shhh, not now*, I chided my overenthusiastic inner ho, who was lusting after Zain.

"Yeah, that sounds good. I'm glad you're not one for small talk. I love girls who are direct." Pete's hand almost grazed my arm when someone tugged him from behind.

I didn't know whether to heave a sigh of relief or yell at Zain, who had interrupted Pete. "Bro, sorry, it was an accident."

"No problem." Pete nodded and turned back. "So..."

"Ah... my drink. I mean, I'll have some water. Can you just..." I interrupted Pete this time.

I could see Pete stifle his frustration at yet another interruption before he ordered some sparkling water. He placed the glass in front of me and leaned forward. "Like I was saying, it's a refreshing change to see someone who gets to the point. I love dating apps, man. Works perfectly well for casual sex, don't you think?" He sipped his beer while I felt my eyes widen endlessly.

"Casual... se—"

"Bro, that girl over there is waving at you."

Pete turned towards Zain, this time annoyance clearly written on his face. "Hey, look—"

"There! Look!" Zain rudely interrupted Pete and signaled toward the lady, who took it as a sign to come forward.

As soon as the woman started talking to Pete, it was clear that they'd hooked up in the recent past. Placing my glass with a thud on the counter, I stood up. It was one thing to disregard my preferences, but to move on from one woman to the next so casually, I knew that just wasn't for me.

Annoyed with the whole online dating scene, I took my purse from the counter. "Pete, looks like you have more than one date for the evening. Let me make your life easy. Enjoy the evening with her." Without looking back at Zain, I flounced out of the restaurant.

"Wait... What? What's your name? Preethi? Parineeti?"

"Pari!" I heard Zain mock Pete before throwing some bills on the counter. "And don't you dare follow her out. The only reason my fist hasn't connected with you is out of respect for her. This was a mistake. One that she won't repeat."

I fumed at the entire exchange, wanting to kill both Zain and Pete. The minute I walked out of the restaurant, I sensed Zain behind me. I barely had time to think before he whirled me around.

"I'll follow you home." It wasn't a request or a question.

"No."

I blanched when he came forward and whispered into my ear in an icy tone. "If you don't want me to spank your adorable ass right here, you'll get into your car and get home safe."

His tone and his words created a throbbing in my core. Suppressing my body's reaction, I flounced once more, this time walking away from Zain.

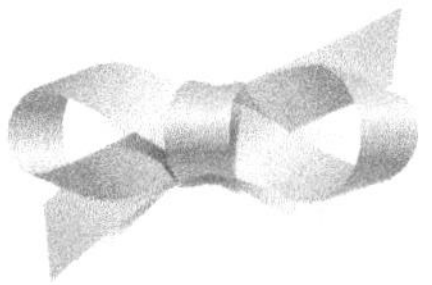

Zain

I watched her sway her cute behind and walk towards her car. Seeing her sexy-as-fuck dress, I was ready to spank my angel's delectable ass for going out on a random date with a creep. I gritted my teeth until the urge passed and got into my car. The minute she got out of the car and walked towards the back door, I caught up with her. Thankfully, John had dropped her before driving the car into the garage.

"Hold on!"

"No!"

With anyone else, the dismissal would have turned me icy cold, but my angel only turned me on. "Not so fast." I caught her wrist and whirled her around before pushing her against the wall beside the door that directly opened into the kitchen.

"Will you stop manhandling me?" she hissed.

"If I wasn't furious with your fucking idea of a date, I'd find your angry face cute and amusing." I didn't care that I was practically growling.

"It's my life, my choice, my date, and I can do anything I want."

"Not while I'm alive. You will fucking not go out on any more random dates. I'll kill anyone who treats you without respect." I was satisfied to see her pupils dilate and her breathing turn erratic. I Imm. I enjoyed knowing Pari wasn't as unaffected as she liked to pretend.

"Why? You don't own me."

That minx. She then shrugged after delivering that sassy comeback. As if she didn't know or didn't care. Two could play this game. "Don't I?" My voice deepened, making her shiver with awareness. Good! My hand moved from her wrist, up her bare arm, to touch her pulse point, where I could feel her pulse racing. My other hand caught the bare patch of skin beneath her crop top, caressing the silvery patch of skin with lazy movements.

I felt her stiffen and bite her lip when my hand grazed beneath the crop top. "No... yes... I don't know." I hardly heard her whisper. My gaze was focused on her dark eyes that traced my lips with hunger.

"Casual sex for your first time? Really?" Despite the temptation standing in front of me, my anger returned. Did she not care about her own safety? I felt her shiver and loosened my grip marginally.

"I didn't... know. I thought it was a regular date. You know, where we'd have a coffee or a drink and some... conversation. I didn't think beyond that. I swear!"

When I saw genuine fear crowd my angel's eyes, I softened a little.

"Anyway, it's all your fault," she declared.

I raised a brow. "How's this hairbrained idea my fault?"

"You kissed me and wouldn't... wouldn't text or call me for seven whole days. I've never done... anything. Dates, kissing, nothing! I don't know the rules, don't know what to expect—"

My lips cut her words off mid-sentence. I couldn't stand and do nothing when her eyes were begging me to teach her to kiss, to date, to... fuck! I was done hearing nonsense about why she should see other men. Any rules or doubts or whatever she wanted to figure out, I was confident she'd do it her own way. Hell, she should make her own rules. Like a queen.

When my lips parted hers, she gave in without a murmur, raising the heat by several notches. I pulled her closer, simultaneously thrusting my tongue into her mouth. That's when I heard a soft moan escape her lips. Immediately, I pushed her into the wall with my body, deepening the kiss and sucking her tongue.

Only the fact that we were at her parents' place stopped me from tearing her clothes off and taking her against the wall. Shit! Now that the image formed behind my eyes, I couldn't purge it. I was a thirty-year-old man but could only hope I didn't embarrass myself like a teenage boy.

Sensing my point of no return, I eased away a little, trying to move away from the tempting little minx.

"Zain, don't stop," she whimpered.

I could feel her death grip on my shirt. My girl was going to leave marks when the time came, I thought with satisfaction.

"I want you," she breathed.

I swallowed hard when she went on her tiptoes to reach for my lips. Her nipples were hard, and they brushed against my chest, almost unraveling me completely. Dear God, she wasn't making it easy on me. Not at all!

"Wait," I panted. "Angel, you gotta stop if you don't want me to take you here," I begged, my eyes pleading.

I saw her gasp even as a pretty blush covered her cheeks. "Oh!" Her disorientation was adorable. "I don't know what came over me," she whispered, as if she was too scared to say it out. The word *desire*.

I felt her withdraw and caught her cheek in my palm. "No, don't be shy with me. Not after what happened now." I caressed her soft skin. "If you really want to go out on a date, I'll take you out on a proper date. This time, it'll be the right way. One date. So? What do you say?"

I could see her waver for a moment before she decided. "Okay," she answered with a smile.

I kissed her knuckles gently. "Ciao, angel. I'll text you the details. Go in before I'm tempted to kidnap you. And no other blind dates or any dates. Got it?" I reminded her gruffly, disturbed at the prospect of another man with Pari.

"I don't want any other man." She answered with a glint in her eyes, lifting her chin up.

I pulled her back and kissed her hard. Once. "You gotta stop throwing out such parting statements, baby. My control is wearing thin already." I smiled when I saw Pari blush before she skipped inside after blowing me a kiss.

Brat! After the disastrous evening, my breath eased for the first time in hours. One date. One date was all I'd promised and I would definitely make it count, I vowed to myself as I turned around and walked to my car.

#6

Pari

My heart was racing, and my excitement was through the roof. It was time for my date with Zain! A smile hovered on my lips at my surprise date, which I knew nothing about. After the dating app fiasco two days ago, I was really looking forward to this. This time, somehow, it felt right. As if this was meant to be.

I checked my appearance in the mirror once more. My pink dress and my black pumps were on point. I inspected my mom's pink Jimmy Choo shoes, which had a cute bow at the back. I conveniently stole this pair from her for my date. Of course, I did! Who needs fifty freaking pairs of shoes, anyway? Apparently, Tanya Grover does. Thankfully, her shoe size and mine matched. Which meant her hoarding tendency benefitted me during times like these.

"Darling, you look so pretty."

I turned around to face my mom, who'd quietly entered my room. "Mom, I didn't hear you come in."

She smiled before hugging me. "My baby girl is all grown up."

Immediately, I heard her sniffle. "Mom, not the waterworks. Not now! Please," I begged, knowing I'd also tear up if she cried.

"Oh, all right. These shoes look great too. I have good taste." She shrugged and gave a watery giggle.

I rolled my eyes and smiled at her. My mom was one of those amazing women who could kick up a storm in a boardroom and be a kick-ass mother all at the same time. This tiny woman now focused only on the philanthropic side of my dad's company. Despite being wealthy by her own merits and being the wife of one of the richest men in the country, she ensured Navin and I had a normal childhood. I broke out of my thoughts when she continued speaking.

"Anyway, I came to check if you were okay with the whole thing. I wanted to remind you not to put up with shit from any man. Even Zain. If he doesn't treat you like a queen, he doesn't deserve you. Understood?"

"Yes, Mom. I want what you and Dad have. I don't think I'd settle for anything less."

"I'm glad to hear that, honey. You're the shining star when you walk into a room, and you deserve nothing but the best. If you ever want to talk, I'm right here, my sunshine." My mom kissed my cheek before leaving my room.

Thanking my lucky stars I was blessed with great parents, I put on my black cardigan over my pink dress and left my room. The minute I stepped out of the main door, I saw Zain's black SUV enter the gate. Smiling, I walked forward, suddenly feeling nervousness overtaking my earlier excitement.

After my outburst about not having a clue about relationships, Zain had texted me that same night. We've been texting ever since, our conversations laced with banter and serious talks. Although he hadn't really gone too personal with his past, the little nothings still lifted my spirits. Immensely!

And so far, whatever he'd revealed about himself, I liked. Of course, Zain being Zain, he'd type a few words against my barrage of texts.

"Angel, you're looking beautiful." Zain's eyes traveled from my head to my toes as soon as he got out of the car.

I felt my face flush at his compliment. Seeing my reaction to his words, he smirked before pecking me on my cheek. Zain opened the door for me and buckled me in before going around and getting into the driver's seat.

"Where are we going?" I knew I was practically buzzing with excitement, but I couldn't help it. I was bad at both keeping and waiting for surprises.

"You'll see."

I almost swooned when he took my hand and placed a soft kiss on my knuckles. I took a shuddering breath and tried not to think about our kiss. Will there be more today? I snuck a sideways glance at him, noticing his biceps and his veiny forearms. Oooh!

Kiara and I always agreed that there was something insanely sexy about a man driving his car with ease and confidence. Add some muscular forearms with visible veins and it was hotttt. I exhaled forcefully. Was the AC on in the car?

"You okay?"

I nodded immediately, praying he wouldn't sense my naughty thoughts about him. Mercifully, he let it go after throwing me a piercing glance. Wisely, I looked away for the remainder of the drive, not wanting to think about his hands, lips, or any body part.

Fifteen minutes later, my breath caught in my throat when Zain stopped in front of my favorite bookstore. It was one of my favorite places to visit and I couldn't have asked for a better place for our first outing.

"Oh! I love this place. Thank you for bringing me here."

Zain gave me a look that said he was aware. "Come on, let's get in. I have a lot of things lined up for us today."

I tried not to gape. "There's more?" My eyes widened.

"Surprise, remember? Now, come on."

I placed my hand in his much bigger one and walked into the beautiful stone building hand in hand with Zain.

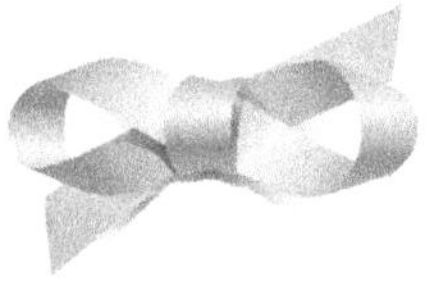

Zain

I heaved a sigh of relief when I saw Pari's excitement and happiness at seeing the bookstore. Yeah, I'd done my research; I'd hounded my brother until he'd confessed all of Pari's weaknesses, favorite haunts, and likes. I was armed. What can I say? After the colossal fuck-up where I'd unwittingly pushed her into a blind date, I wanted to do better. I only hoped I had the sense and control to stop after the date and show her how she deserved to be treated.

Getting into the huge building, I let her lead the way, trying not to grin when I saw the obvious excitement running through her curvy little body. I'd give anything to see her eyes light up the way they did whenever her eyes landed on one of her favorite books. As she strolled through the aisles, I walked along, content to be in her presence.

She excited and calmed me in a way that was contradictory yet made perfect sense. It wasn't just my body that jumped in her presence. My soul, too, seemed to recognize her. Her light shot through the layer of darkness that had always enveloped me, penetrating to my soul, and humbling me. Was it scary? Of course! But it was also addictive and compelling, pulling me in deeper and deeper.

"Oh, I love this book."

I glanced at Pari and noticed she had a classic by Jane Austen in her hand.

"This one too..." Her voice trailed away as she walked from one aisle to another. "What do you like? Wait, do you even like reading?" She turned around to offer a quick glance at me.

"Yes. I stick to biographies, business, and technology. Mostly."

"Oh!" Her dismayed expression was adorable.

"If it helps, I could start reading spicy romance. Whips and Mr. Grey, anyone?" My lips twitched when she hit my chest playfully.

"Shut up! You think you know all about it, but the book you're referring to is nothing. There's alien romance, paranormal, and werewolves..."

"Whoa, whoa! Okay, I give up. I'll stick to my genres for now. For what it's worth, I prefer doing it instead of reading about it." I shrugged.

"Zain!" she gasped and looked around frantically, seeing if anyone had overheard our conversation.

A chortle escaped my lips at the crimson that scorched her face. She really was adorable and wore her heart on her sleeve. Smiling, I took the books from her hand and strolled around until she was done. After paying for her books, I led her to a bench beneath a gigantic banyan tree.

Placing her books in my car, I surreptitiously opened my electric cooler to whip out her favorite coffee shake laced with sea salt and caramel. When I handed her the cup, she literally squealed.

"Oh, my god! This is my favorite. Thank you so so much. Everything's just so... perfect," Pari confessed excitedly.

I smiled before sitting down beside my angel, touched by her response. She was practically an heiress and could easily afford the company that produced the damn coffee. Yet she was happy with the little things. Somehow, life and its ugliness seemed to have left her alone. I prayed my darkness wouldn't touch her charming naivety. It wouldn't. Not if I stayed away.

"I'm glad you're enjoying our outing. For the record, this is how you're supposed to be courted and not like that asshole you went out with," I grumbled.

She placed her hand on mine. "Don't frown, and I'm sorry. I didn't mean to worry you the other day. I honestly had no clue about these dating apps work. In fact, it was Kiara who suggested I sign up for a dating site." She sighed, sipping her drink.

"Well, no more dating apps or dating strange men, okay?" I didn't want to sound like a possessive asshole, but the truth was, I was one. I was concerned about her naivety. No wonder Uncle Neil was protective of her.

Shifting closer, I was about to check if she was comfortable when she turned to me to kiss me gently on my mouth. I stilled. Jesus Christ, she was one sweet little thing. And this was the first time she'd kissed me of her own will. My blood pounded in my veins, traveling south to make my dick rock hard. With supreme effort, I remained still, allowing her shy exploration.

A sound nearby made her draw back with a small gasp, emphasizing her inexperience and our nine-year age gap. More than ever, I felt like a bastard for wanting her at that moment. Knowing I didn't deserve her and not caring one bit, I continued to bask in her presence, content to hear her soft voice and enjoy her shy touch.

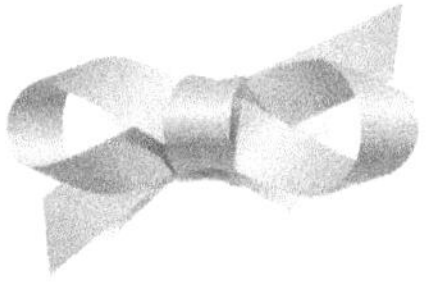

#7

Pari

It had been an hour on the bench and the October weather in Bangalore was ideal for outdoors—pleasant, lightly windy, and not very sunny. As I continued to chat with Zain, for the first time in my life, my thoughts and words flowed easily without my usual overthinking.

I thoroughly enjoyed speaking to Zain about my family, my art, the doodling I did, and my dreams and aspirations to open an art-related business. All the while, he listened without blinking, staring into my eyes as if he were fascinated with every word that came out of my mouth. That was probably the reason I didn't notice the sun going down or the colors of dusk setting in.

As a slight breeze caressed my skin, I realized materialistic things had little to do with true happiness. It really warmed my heart, knowing Zain hadn't tried to take me out to a fancy restaurant or an outrageously expensive date. I would have been really disappointed if he'd taken me for a helicopter ride or something.

Zain seemed to know what truly mattered, what would make me comfortable. I felt a pang when it occurred to me he'd committed only to one date. The realization chilled me, making me shiver.

Noticing my shiver, Zain stood up, gently pulling me up with him. "It's getting cold. Shall we leave? We have one last stop before I take you home."

"Of course!" I stood up with a small smile. "Once again, thanks so much, Zain. Everything was just so... perfect!" My smile widened, and I didn't care that my feelings were out there. I didn't believe in hiding and pretense; why start now?

Zain's eyes darkened at my words and he said nothing. Caressing his thumb over the pulse on my wrist, he led me towards his SUV. Acutely aware of his fingers that were intertwined with mine, I followed him mutely, enjoying his touch. Very well knowing it was temporary. Knowing it would lead to heartbreak.

The minute the car doors closed, a zing of awareness passed through my body. Zain's muscular form next to me, his scent, everything about him, threatened to consume me, the sensory overload rattling my nerves. I wasn't sure where he was taking me, but something told me we'd be alone.

Biting my lower lip, I looked out the window. Will I be able to keep my hands off him? The other times we'd kissed, it was Zain who'd stopped. Would he stop if we kissed this time, too? What if he didn't? Was I ready to take the next step? A tiny voice inside me warned there was no going back once I gave myself to him. I released my lip, hoping my face didn't betray my worry.

"You seem to be a little tense." Zain threw a sideways glance at me, his eyes zeroing in on the rapid rise and fall of my chest before glancing at my fingers that were fidgeting.

I shook my head. My mouth was dry, and words were lost on me. Before he could quiz me, he slowed down. I breathed out in relief when he stopped in front of a beautiful house. Looking at the sight of the stone wall and the rustic exterior, I forgot all about my internal dilemma and admired the house in front of me.

"Wow, this place looks stunning. Whose is it?" I didn't wait for him to open the door as I jumped out, eager to explore.

"It's mine. Umm, I stumbled on this property two years ago when I was driving along this road. It took me all this time to convince the previous owner to sell. I officially bought this property two months ago, but the renovations are still going on. The guest rooms are pending. That's the reason I haven't moved in here yet. Come on in."

Zain caught my small hand in his much bigger one and led me inside. The moment I stepped inside, I caught my breath in awe. "Wow... this... it's so beautiful, Zain." I looked around, taking it all in.

The living room looked cozy, with a set of French doors leading to a beautiful garden. The entire room was spacious, charming, and warm, with pastels and greens. To my delight, the design seemed to be inspired by French countryside houses. I didn't realize my eyes were shining, nor did I notice the closed door behind us.

"I agree."

My eyes met Zain's, and I blushed when I realized he was looking at me as he uttered those words. I walked away from him, afraid he'd hear the loud drumming of my heartbeat. His very presence was potent, reducing me to a blubbering mess. By now, I was sure about my feelings, but what if I was simply a passing phase for him? I was startled when he spoke, turning around to face him at last.

"Dinner? I have your favorites, and I can heat them up quickly."

I didn't realize he'd stepped closer. His spicy cologne invaded my senses, making me want things. Naughty things that didn't involve food. With some effort, I made my voice work.

"Oh, thank you so much. This is a lot of effort..." I trailed off, not sure how to convey my feelings. He was the first man who'd attempted to please me without expecting anything in return. It didn't matter to him I was *the* Neil Grover's daughter. He saw me, Pari, a shy, bookish nerd with a penchant for doodling and making desserts.

"My pleasure, angel. Like I said, this is exactly how you should be treated."

I felt a fission of unease at his words. So, this was just a rehearsal then? For me to learn what to expect? Clearing my throat, I walked to the beautiful dining room. Away from him. I couldn't afford to fall for Zain. Not when he clearly said it was just one date. Unaware of my internal struggle, Zain followed me into the room before he set the table for us.

This time, to my surprise, he spoke a lot more than usual. He showed me some of his designs and his ideas for sustainable buildings. His passion was to build a better world for everyone around him.

Hearing him share his dreams and desires, all my defenses broke. How could I resist this perfect man? It wasn't fair that I was falling for someone who wasn't into relationships. Ignoring the melancholic thoughts, I enjoyed the meal and his company, willing this date to never end.

An hour later, I put my napkin aside with a contented sigh. "I don't think I can eat another bite. It was delicious." He'd arranged for enchiladas and a beautiful and colorful Mexican burrito bowl. My absolute favorites!

"Ah, we have just one last thing remaining." Zain got up and extended a hand towards me. Curious, I took his hand and moved with him, eager for the next surprise.

When he opened the door that led to the garden, I stepped into what could easily be an alternate universe. The beautiful lawn was filled with the fragrance of jasmine. On one side, a blanket was spread out, and by the side lay a cooler. A couple of lanterns cast a warm glow on the whole setup, making it almost seem magical.

"Am I dreaming?" I blinked rapidly before turning towards Zain.

"I hope not. The best part is waiting to be enjoyed." He pointed to the cooler. "Dessert!"

My heartbeat picked up when his eyes zoomed in on my lips. I inhaled with a shudder and moved toward the blanket. Kicking off my heels, I sat down with a blissful sigh. Zain followed me after unpacking the dessert.

Yet another favorite of mine. I wondered who spilled all my likes to him. Before I could pick up the spoon, Zain beat me to it. He held the ice-cold dessert near my mouth, waiting for me to open. I did. And the resulting taste was an explosion of heaven in my mouth. I closed my eyes and moaned softly, enjoying the flavors and textures.

"Fuck!"

I peeled my eyes open to see something dark flash in Zain's eyes. Dropping the spoon, he pulled me onto his lap.

"Wh... what are you doing?" My breathless whisper turned into a whimper when I felt his tongue lick some ice cream from the corner of my mouth.

"Eating my dessert," he murmured with a sexy grunt. I clutched his shoulders as he nuzzled the spot between my neck and shoulder.

I was wrong earlier. This! This was heaven. Before I could think any further, Zain's lips captured mine in a long, deep kiss. The dessert was abandoned, and I didn't know when or how I got horizontal with Zain on top. The breath whooshed out of my body the minute he moved on top of me. Zain supported himself on his forearms, his lips almost touching mine.

"Please tell me you want this, angel."

I nodded, thrilled to hear the longing beneath his hoarse plea.

"I need to hear you say it," he insisted, his gray eyes boring into mine.

"Yes. I want you. This. Us," I murmured, clutching his shirt.

No sooner did those words leave my lips, he possessed my lips again with a swiftness that left my head reeling. I didn't realize how much I wanted this connection with him, until he kissed me again. I arched up, a soft moan involuntarily escaping me as his tongue plundered my mouth. His hands held mine over my head as his tongue continued to weave magic inside my mouth.

"I've been dying to taste you again," he growled into my ear.

A spark of something wanton passed through me at his possessive growl. "Me too," I whispered hesitantly. I gulped when I saw his eyes morph into dark pools of desire at my words.

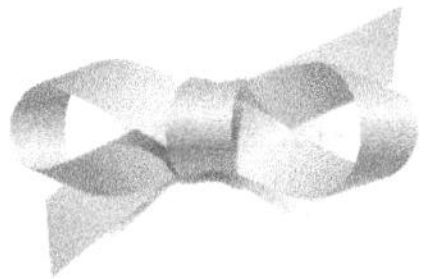

Zain

Through the evening, I'd tried to stay away. Even didn't react when she'd kissed me. But after hours in her company, my body was tired of fighting. Seeing her lick the dessert, I couldn't resist my angel any longer. Especially when she had that look in her eyes, full of longing, melancholy, and lust. Her eyes mirrored her heart, and when she looked at me with such want, I couldn't help but act on it.

She reduced me to a horny mess without even trying. For once, I didn't care about that voice at the back of my head that always taunted me. The same voice that mocked me, reminding me I wasn't enough. I forcefully subdued that voice and trailed my lips along her neck, and below, to her pulse point.

Skillfully removing her cardigan and tugging down the straps of her dress and bra, I took a moment to enjoy her porcelain skin. Her curvy, voluptuous breasts fit just right in my large hands, rivaling her wide hips and her thick thighs that were made for a man like me.

Pari made a soft sound and tried to move away, shying away from my gaze. I was having none of that. Biting my fingers into the soft flesh of her hips, I tipped her chin with my other hand. "You're beautiful, angel. I'm honored to see you. The real you. Don't hide yourself from me."

Her breath caught at my words, and I saw her eyes water. Shit! I felt like a lowlife when I saw her tears. Gently wiping her tears, I bent down to bite her shoulder before tracing my lips over the swell of her breasts. Feeling my angel squirm, I smiled against her skin. She was restless, trying to reach for something. Ah! The unknown... for her. Lucky for her, I knew what she wanted.

Cupping one of her breasts, I moved my lips to capture the other one. Immediately, I felt her stiffen before she arched into me, offering herself to me.

"Good girl," I appreciated her initiative. I loved the fact that she wasn't being shy with me anymore.

Her movements stilled at once, and she looked at me with wide eyes. "Why do those words sound so good?" She moaned.

"Because you are one. A good girl. MY good girl. And your body knows it." This time, I switched to the other peak and suckled her without mercy. I was done with slow. Yes, she wasn't used to making love, sex... whatever it was called, but there was always a first time. With me. Only me.

"Whatever you do feels so good," Pari confessed breathlessly. "I... I want something... more. Please."

She wasn't sure what her body was begging her for. But I knew. I knew exactly what she wanted. I continued to tease her, driving her mindless with pleasure. When I felt her hands claw my back before trying to reach for my shirt buttons, I groaned. She could tip me off the charts so easily, and she wasn't even aware of her powers. Thank God for that!

I moved up to kiss her hard. Once. Taking her small hands and placing them on my shirt, I grunted. "Undress me." Her shocked gasp surprised me. Didn't she want to do it anyway just a minute ago?

She quickly recovered. "Yeah, okay," Pari whispered shakily, immediately starting on the first button.

I tried not to growl when she wet her lips with her tongue. Moving away slightly to give her some room, I noticed her fingers were shaking. Mercifully, her fingers turned deft after a brief struggle. The moment she pushed my shirt off my shoulders, I went back to her, groaning at the sensation of skin on skin. With her mussed hair and her swollen lips, she was way too sexy for her own good, and the thought of restraint ceased to exist.

I bunched up her half-undone dress to her waist, wanting to tear it off completely. Lightly grazing my finger over her lacy briefs, I murmured with satisfaction when a startled moan escaped her lips.

"Ple... please be gentle..." At her breathless whisper, I paused.

I knew I'd be her first. Yet, hearing her confess her inexperience did something to me. I tried not to act like a caveman. She was so precious, and this was a gift I'd cherish for life.

"I know. Thank you, precious." I was grateful for the opportunity to be her first. I'd never take that for granted.

Trailing my lips over her shoulder, I inched my fingers towards her core. A curse tore out of my mouth when my fingers moved underneath the fabric to feel her wet heat.

"Zain!" Her shocked exclamation did nothing to stop me.

"Yes! It's Zain and only Zain," I drawled, looking into her molten eyes.

"Do that again."

I chuckled at her angry demand, enjoying the way her eyes came alive with want. She looked stunning with her desire-filled eyes and her delectable curves. Her flushed look, messy hair, and her impatience to be mine only enhanced her allure, beckoning me to her like a moth to a flame.

Kissing her, I probed her, enjoying the way her tight channel gripped me. Pari let out a mewl, clutching my biceps in a tight grip. Taking that as encouragement, I went back to her folds, swiping my thumb over the bundle of nerves.

"Oh!" She began squirming after letting out a shocked exclamation. Moving my lips to her peak, I caught her hips with my hands, steadying her beneath me.

"Don't move," I commanded, before playing with her nipples using my tongue. As I increased the speed and pressure, I felt her folds weeping, her juices coating my finger. Murmuring in satisfaction, I suckled harder, uncaring if it left a mark. Grunting in satisfaction, I wished I could have this every day. I'd die a lucky man.

My thoughts broke apart when Pari let out a sharp cry, her hands clutching me tighter. She was close. Closing my eyes, I licked between her peaks before introducing another finger. When I added a scissoring motion, I felt her legs tremble even as she whimpered helplessly. For a moment, her entire body stilled before she convulsed with a soundless cry. I felt her tight channel milk my fingers, gentling my efforts gradually as the spasms reduced to nothing.

Eventually, when her body slumped, I raised my eyes, thrilled to see a very satisfied Pari lying back with her eyes closed.

Hurriedly, my hands reached down to my zipper, when the doorbell rang. I froze for a couple of seconds before uttering a terse curse. Righting my clothes and Pari's, I moved away hurriedly. That's when Pari's eyes shot open and she looked at me with confusion and hesitation.

"I'm sorry, angel. I don't know who is bothering us at this hour. Few know about this property." I knew I was growling, but the nagging feeling inside me almost told me who was waiting on the other side of the door even before I got up to open it.

Just as I'd suspected, the minute I opened the door, I looked into the face of the one woman who had made my life hell. My birth mother. "What are you doing here at this hour?" I didn't give a fuck if I sounded rude. I wanted this woman away from my angel. Pari was too pure for this woman's shit.

"Come on, son. Is this any way to greet your mother? Oh, and is this a new friend of yours?" She waved at Pari, who smiled back tentatively. Obviously, my angel didn't know what to make of this situation.

"Pari, can you please give us a moment? I'll be with you shortly."

"Umm... it's getting late. Why don't I wait in your car? I'd like to leave; if you're okay with that," she whispered to me, her eyes darting between my mother and me.

"Sounds good." I nodded, the excitement and red-hot desire of the past hour crashing abruptly.

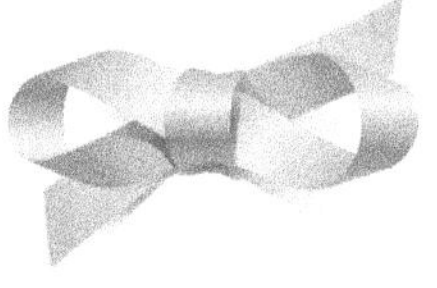

#8

Pari

After ten agonizing minutes of waiting, I saw Zain and his mother come out of his place. My shock hadn't entirely abated from seeing his birth mom. She was a slender woman with auburn hair, and she looked beautiful. Exquisite. No wonder Zain was also a looker, I thought to myself. I didn't realize she was a part of Zain's life. After his outburst the other day, I didn't dare pry into this side of his life. Despite this interruption, I told myself I wouldn't probe without him initiating the conversation first. I watched his mom get into a waiting cab before he walked towards the car.

The minute he got into the driver's seat of his SUV, I could sense the chillness coming off him. I shivered unconsciously, noticing his rigidity in his jaw and the unmistakable coldness in his gray eyes. He didn't look at me. Not once. Gone was the warm lover who had worshiped my body just minutes before his mother had arrived. I tried my best not to react in front of him, but he was making it damn hard for me to retain my composure.

I told myself it wasn't my fault his mom interrupted our wonderful date. But even in my head, my conviction sounded feeble. All too soon, before I could broach the elephant in the car, we reached my place. The perfect gentleman that he was,

Zain got out to open the door and walk me up to the front door. I opened my mouth to speak. Only his lips stopped my words with a quick hard kiss, leaving me breathless.

I forced down my nervousness and stuttered out the words. "I loved the date. Thank you for everything, Zain." If anything, my whisper only seemed to agonize him more.

He nodded. "I'm sorry about the way it ended, though." He paused and looked into my eyes with a solemn expression. "Goodnight, angel."

I felt my eyes water when I heard the finality in his voice. Somehow, it didn't seem like goodnight. It sounded more like goodbye. One date. That was all he promised, and he'd given me more than I could ask for.

"Goodnight," I whispered back, my heart in my throat. When I'd entered his place, I never thought the evening would end in this manner. But then, fate had other plans. Which truly sucked. Because I loved being with Zain. I loved Zain. My breath hitched at the enormity of thinking those words. I turned away from him swiftly, wanting to get away before I did something stupid, like blurting out my love.

Once inside, I immediately went up to my room and closed the door behind me. I loved Zain. His kisses were off the charts, and my body melted for him every single time. Instinctively, I knew what I felt went beyond physical intimacy.

I hadn't even been remotely tempted by any other guy so far. With Zain, it had been instant and exciting from the moment I laid eyes on him. My body, mind, and soul recognized him in a way I couldn't comprehend. Groaning in frustration at the whole thing, I peeled off my dress to get into my comfy clothes.

In the end, I hoped and prayed Zain would work out his demons and reach out to me. His relationship with his biological parents and his life before his adoption would always be a sword hanging above us. Until he attempted to heal and work on himself, we could have no semblance of a relationship. Inhaling a shuddering breath, I told myself to believe that he'd come back to me. I had to! I didn't have any other choice, did I?

. . ⁓ . .

ONE WEEK LATER, I WASN'T sure what to believe anymore. After the magical date that had ended not-so-magically, Zain had ghosted me. Yet again! I didn't know whether to throw something in frustration or cry in distress. I wondered, not for the first time, if this is what a relationship with Zain would be like. A few magical moments followed by tense silence until the next time he got in touch with me.

The minute these thoughts crossed my mind, I felt myself shrivel. Whether or not he realized it, what he was putting me through was emotional abuse—pure and simple. How else could I describe this emotional seesaw? Along with frustration, I felt anger rise for the first time in a week. Heartbreak was a bitch, and I wasn't someone who liked to dwell on negative emotions.

Picking up my phone, I dialed Zain's number. It went directly to his voicemail. Disconnecting the call, I dialed Aarav's number instead.

"Yo! How are you, babe?" Aarav picked up the call on the second ring.

I wished for the thousandth time Zain was as easygoing as Aarav. My stupid heart and body only wanted that grumpy man with mommy issues.

"Not good. Not good at all. Can you meet me at my place?"

When Aarav heard the crack in my voice, he immediately turned serious. "Hey, are you okay? Shit! Don't cry... please. I'm coming right away."

I sniffled and nodded, not realizing Aarav couldn't see me nodding over the phone.

Barely fifteen minutes later, Aarav barged into my room without bothering to knock. Well, he didn't need to most times. We were best friends, who were also like siblings, and he was as dear to me as Navin.

"Shit, bro, what happened? You okay? You look like death." Aarav frowned at me.

"I feel like it."

"Why? What happened?"

"It's your stupid, obnoxious brother," I snapped, targeting my anger on the wrong person.

"Zain? Last I heard, he was planning for some epic date, right? You guys didn't go out?" Predictably, Aarav was taken aback by my reaction.

"Oh, we went out all right," I replied bitterly, pulling him on to my bed. We both sat down facing each other before I started narrating the entire saga. Once I started, I couldn't stop. The entire story right from my first meeting with Zain tumbled out. I left the intimate parts out, knowing it was too personal to share with another person. I was pretty sure Aarav wouldn't want to hear about his brother's sex life, anyway.

"Bruh, this is insane. I didn't realize my brother was such a tool. Man!" He ran a hand through his hair.

"Tell me about it." I rolled my watery eyes. "Why couldn't I have fallen for you instead?" I giggled when I saw Aarav scrunch his nose in disgust.

"Dude, that's gross. You're like my sister."

"I know, you idiot!" Now that I had off-loaded all my frustration with my buddy, I felt lighter. "I think I'm hangry." I gave him a small grin.

Aarav shook his head in exasperation. "You're nuts. Wait, let me order something. We'll watch something sic, okay?"

"'Kay." I settled down on the bed comfortably, snatching the phone from his hands to choose my order.

"Sorry, bro. Didn't realize Zain had so much going on. And his contact with his birth mom, not sure if my parents know about it." He looked hesitant and uncomfortable at the prospect of secrets.

"Oh! Do you think your mom and dad will be bothered if they find out about it?"

"I don't know. But the bigger issue is Zain's reaction to her."

"Well, you know what? I cannot live Zain's life for him. If he doesn't want me..." I broke off, swallowing my tears before continuing. "It's awful, but not the end of the world. I don't want a man who cannot see my worth," I declared, ignoring my heart that broke all over again.

I noticed Aarav glance at me with worry. He remained quiet, and eventually we settled down to watch a series we both enjoyed.

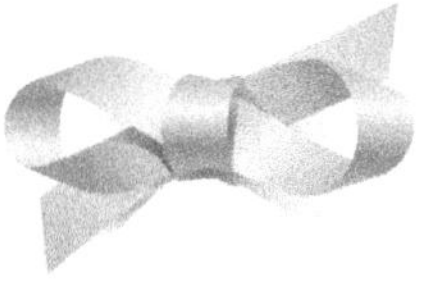

Zain

I looked up from my desk to see my mom enter my room. "Mom?" I was working from home. Actually, I was only working, be it in the office or at home. Nothing else seemed to matter. It had been nearly nine days since the visit from my birth mother. Thanks to her, I haven't been the same ever since.

"Are you okay, honey?"

I cleared my throat and nodded. "Yeah. Do you need anything, Mom?"

I watched my mom sit on the couch beside my workstation with a sigh. "Papa and I are worried about you, sweetheart. You haven't been yourself these last few days. Did you think we wouldn't notice?"

"I'm perfectly fine, and nothing's wrong with me." I frowned, hating all the attention. My head wasn't in the right place to deal with more guilt.

"Do you want to reconnect with your family, honey?" My mom was soft-spoken and looked meek, but underneath that soft exterior she had a spine of steel that always took people by surprise.

"Mom! No, I mean, I was glad to get out of that hellhole. You know that, Ma."

"I know, sweetie. I know. I've just been so worried about you." She got up to hug me, making me swallow the emotions that threatened to burst out.

"My mother has been in contact with me for the last few years," I blurted out the truth, knowing it would hurt my mom if I continued to hide things from her.

She nodded, as if she already knew that. I hoped the shock I felt wasn't visible on my face.

"Are you okay with that? Why didn't you talk to us about this sooner, Zain? Did you feel that your Papa or I might stop you from seeing her?"

When her eyes glistened with tears, I got up from my desk and sat next to her on the couch, holding her in my embrace. I'd hidden the whole thing to avoid hurting my mom. For all my noble intentions, I seemed to cause a lot of pain. Precisely what I'd wanted to avoid. "Not at all! Mom, I'm sorry. It's not what you think. I didn't want that woman and her filth to touch you all. Especially you." *And Pari*, I thought to myself.

"Zain!" Mom looked shocked before she recovered. "Is that what you've thought all these years?" She caressed my cheek. "Oh, my dear boy. You're one of the most sensitive, beautiful souls I've had the fortune to meet. Nothing and no one can diminish your light. Don't allow anyone to, honey."

My dad quietly came in and held my mom, glancing above her head into my gray eyes. "Zain, look, we are family. There's nothing you cannot tell us. Got it?"

"Yes, Dad."

"We don't care when you joined us. You're our son, and that's that. You just... happened. You completed our family; you were meant to be." My mom looked up with a fierce expression, her protective instincts rapidly rising.

"And you can see your birth parents anytime you want. But if you don't want to, then you don't have to. Guilt, especially misplaced guilt, is a very heavy burden, son. Perhaps it's time to shed it off your shoulders." This time, it was my dad who spoke in an unusually quiet voice. For a man with a lot of flamboyance, he was deep and emotional underneath.

"Thanks, Dad. I love you both," I replied in a gruff voice, my throat unusually thick with tears.

"Well, you better," my mom threatened with a watery smile. She got up with my dad. "I don't know what's going on, but I'm sure you'll figure it out. We are here for you." She looked at me and hesitated before continuing. "But whatever it is, don't hurt Pari or drag her into all this. She doesn't deserve it."

"Pari?" My dad looked at me in surprise.

"Yes, our Pari. I pray our son gets his head out of his ass before another man steals that beautiful girl away." My mom looked at me with a stern expression although she replied to dad.

I got the hint. It was a subtle warning, and I had no difficulty reading the subtext. Take the time to heal, but don't mess around with Pari in the process.

"Do you like her? Is this serious?" My dad was persistent, wanting to hear it from me directly.

I ran a hand through my hair and sighed. "Yes. No. I don't know."

"You better know your answer to that and soon," he snapped. "Or else, son or not, be prepared to be kicked royally in the ass," my dad growled at me, before walking out of my room with my mom.

I ran a hand down my exhausted face, wishing someone would tell me what to do. With a sigh, I opened my phone and looked at the missed call from my angel. That was two days prior. After that, there was nothing.

Realizing it might not be the best idea, yet wanting to see her, I snatched my car keys and let myself out. I wanted to see Pari. She'd get me. I had to talk to her. Even I realized I couldn't go on like this. Either I had to claim her or let her go. Swallowing, I prayed for courage to do the right thing.

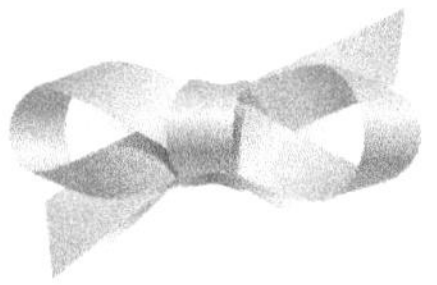

#9

Zain

"Please, talk to me. Just this once." For a man who spoke rarely, I was asking for mercy for the nth time for the day. Predictably, my angel had closed off from me and didn't want to see me. She'd also, apparently, informed my younger brother that she was done with me.

But then, I haven't come up in business or in life by idly watching or accepting the happenings in my life. I was a fighter, and I wanted to speak to her. Knowing her disconnecting my call was what I deserved didn't make it any easier. Fuck! Getting out of my car, I took a chance and pressed the doorbell. When Aunt Tanya opened the door, I was relieved. At least I didn't have to face Uncle Neil, yet.

"You took your time, didn't you?" For once, there was no smile or the signature cheeky grin on Aunt Tanya's face. It bothered me that I was the reason for her solemn face. My stupidity. I let *that* woman get into my head, and now it was coming back to bite me.

"I'm here to make amends. I really want to make it up to her."

Tanya looked into my eyes for a few seconds and sighed. "I suppose everyone deserves one chance, but break my baby's heart once more, and you'll have me to answer to." She nodded, pointing me towards the stairs that led to Pari's room. "And Zain? If you're not sure what you want, I suggest you don't go up those stairs."

"I want to see Pari this once." I repeated in an urgent voice.

Sighing, Aunt Tanya nodded. "I was just leaving for a meeting. Don't break her heart," she warned me again.

"I won't. Thank you," I spoke quietly watching her leave, before turning around, taking the stairs two at a time.

I knocked on Pari's door once and tried the handle. To my relief, the door was unlocked. I stepped in and locked the door for good measure. The minute I stepped in, her vanilla and honey fragrance hit my nostrils, reminding me of our date.

"Zain? What are you doing here? How did you get in?"

I saw Pari come out of the washroom in what could be described as cute-as-fuck pajama shorts and a shirt that had a book and coffee designs on it.

"Zain! Eyes up here," my angel snapped, although a fiery blush covered her cheeks. It was then that I realized I'd been staring at her chest. Not a good way to begin an apology. Clearing my throat, I tried to reach for her hand. Only to have her move it away.

"Angel..."

"My name is not angel." She retorted.

Even her frown was adorable, and I wasn't getting anywhere with that thought. "I know I've fucked up..."

"Damn right you have, and it's not the first time. So stop wasting my time and... and leave." Her words ended on a shaky note. Before she could turn away from me, I caught her wrist.

"Please listen to me."

"Why, Zain? Did you want to hear me when I called you all those times? Despite knowing how much it hurt me the last time you ghosted me. You could have given me a proper closure, at the very least."

"I know, I know. Please, let me explain." I felt like a lowlife when I saw the moisture gather in her dark eyes. Eyes that should have shone with happiness, but were now drenched with tears. All thanks to my royal fuck-up.

"Go away, you're making me cry, and I hate being sad." She sniffled.

"One kiss."

"What?" She looked at me like she couldn't believe my audacity to even suggest such a thing.

"Kiss me once, and if you truly feel nothing, I'll walk away."

"I don't think that's a good idea." She shook her head frantically, her loose knot coming undone, making her silky hair fall to her waist.

Fresh-faced, with her hair down, she truly looked like an angel from heaven. Awestruck by her beauty all over again, I didn't hear her response. Instead, I pulled her towards me and kissed her hard. For a brief second, I felt her stiffen in my arms before her hands went around my neck and she kissed me back.

Picking her up in a single move, I placed her on her bed and joined her immediately. "I've missed you. I've been dying to taste you. If we weren't interrupted the other day, I would have," I murmured, kissing her neck and the base of her throat.

Pari's breath hitched at my words. "This is insane. I don't know if we should do this."

The minute those words came out of her mouth, I gently tugged her lower lip, making her stop. Her body arched up and her tight grip on my shirt contradicted her words, telling me she wanted this as much as I did. My hands immediately got busy, rapidly taking off her shirt. When I saw bare skin beneath, I swore, making my angel whimper softly.

"Perfect. You're perfect," I breathed, caressing her with unsteady hands. My mouth watered at the sight of her perky and round breasts topped with cherry tips. Unable to resist the pull any longer, I bent my head to suckle her. I'd been dying to taste her again, and the reality was far better than the remembered pleasure.

"Zain!" She caught my hair, her hands tightening, silently begging for more.

I tried not to grin triumphantly. She couldn't help it either. She wanted me as much as I wanted her. Perhaps this would convince her to give me another chance. Moving my mouth to the other peak, I gently traced my hands down her chest, to her navel, and below. When I heard her draw a sharp breath, I paused my ministrations to look at her. If she wanted me to stop, I'd stop.

I found her staring at me with wide, desire-filled eyes that were also filled with anticipation this time. She wanted this. I moved my fingers slowly below the elastic and saw her part her legs a little. Atta girl! I bent down to trace a nipple with my tongue. Immediately, Pari mewled and caught the sheet with her hands.

"Shh, baby, calm down."

When my fingers grazed her core, she nearly came off the bed. Fuck! She was primed and ready already. I shouldn't be too surprised. One look at her and my dick was weeping.

Holding her hip with an arm, my mouth and tongue ran over her nipples in circles, teasing and tormenting. Every time I flicked my tongue, I could feel moisture pool around my finger. I brought my finger to my mouth, tasting her, my eyes on her shocked gaze.

"Zain!" Her eyes widened, even as curiosity and awe mingled with desire.

"I fucking love this taste," I declared with a wicked smile.

Seeing her eyes darken with desire, I moved down to peel off her shorts to see her bare, glistening mound. Instinctively, her legs pressed together, making me grasp her thighs to part them. I wanted to taste her and nothing was going to stop me at this moment.

Bending, I took a long swipe, making her cover her mouth with her palm. A small whimper escaped when I swirled my tongue inside. Jesus! She tasted divine and I could go on forever. Settling between her legs, I used my tongue to drive her to the brink of insanity and then some.

I didn't know how long I was buried in her, time and space having lost its meaning. Finally, when she began to move her hips in tune with my movements, I barely stopped the triumphant growl that threatened to escape from my lips.

Instead, I doubled my efforts, wanting her to give in to the madness that plagued the both of us. I would have teased her endlessly; only her cry for help made me pause. Taking pity, I latched my mouth to the bundle of nerves, gently suckling her. When I added a finger into her drenched heat, she thrashed on the bed, her head tossing side to side.

"Zain, I don't know..." Her breathing turned erratic.

Hearing the uncertainty and fear in my angel's voice, I paused momentarily to look into her eyes, encouraging her to let go. "Let go, sweetheart." When I brushed my thumb against her most sensitive place, I felt her stiffen before splintering apart with a silent cry.

Fascinated by her uninhibited response, I kissed her hard and moved my hand one last time over her heated flesh. She flinched, her body way too sensitive after her recent orgasm. I kissed her gently once more before adjusting her clothes. "That was one hell of a kiss, angel."

I frowned when I noticed her eyes awash with tears. "Pari!"

She sat up and righted her clothes completely, her face a strange mixture of satisfaction and pain. "Please leave, Zain."

Her quiet plea broke my heart. "What?" I whispered, watching her expression harden.

"I might be inexperienced, but even I'm aware sexual chemistry alone is not enough to sustain a relationship. And I want it all. The dates, the cuddles, the unconditional support, everything. I cannot live waiting for the next high when you come in and throw in a few orgasms."

"It isn't..." She stopped my words with her hand.

"You wouldn't talk to me after what happened with your mother. I agree, I shouldn't have crossed a line by asking about your biological family. But after your mother interrupted us and you turned all cold, don't you think I deserved an explanation? A better closure, at the very least? I deserved to know if you didn't want me. All that I got was one week of silence. And then... now this. I can't go through this again." Tears swam in her eyes, making me want to hit myself with something for pushing her away.

"I'm sorry, angel. I didn't mean to hurt you." I was practically begging Pari for forgiveness. Yet, somewhere deep in my heart, I already knew I'd lost my sweet angel.

"Goodbye, Zain." Pari's soft voice cut through my heart.

Without replying, I walked out the door, realizing I might have made a monumental blunder.

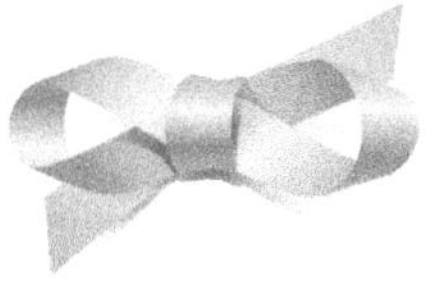

Pari

"Pari, honey, back to earth. Pari!"

I was startled when I heard Aunt Natasha, or Aunt Tasha, as I'd like to call her, call out my name the second time. She was Uncle Arjun's wife and one of my mom's best friends, too. Right now, we were seated in a coffee shop, sipping hot cappuccinos.

"Darling, what's bothering you? You seem to be awfully preoccupied. Is everything okay with you, angel?"

I tried not to blush at that nickname. I could almost hear *his* voice in my ear, rasping that name as he caressed me. His voice and his touch have lingered in my thoughts, making my heart race and my body melt.

Of course, I was trying to forget and move on every single day, but who was I kidding? It wasn't happening anytime soon. Two months and I still yearned for him. My hands hovered over his name on my phone, wanting to hear his voice just once more. I felt the prickle of tears behind my lids when a gnawing ache filled my heart all over again.

"Are those tears?" Aunt Tasha leaned forward with a concerned look. "Is it what I think it is? Involving one Zain?"

"Oh, my god! Does anything ever escape you guys?" I covered my face with my hands, although I was secretly glad I had so many people to fall back on.

"Sweetheart, you know we love you. And be happy Arjun isn't aware of the finer details of your breakup. Yet." She noticed my wince and nodded. "That's right, you and I know how unreasonable my man can be when it comes to you. You'll always be his little girl." She gave me a knowing look that said Zain would be in trouble if Uncle A knew how heartbroken I was.

"But that wasn't why I came to see you, sweetie. I wanted to talk to you about Zain, which is why I've left several important clients waiting and I'm here."

"About Zain? What do you mean, Aunt Tasha?"

"Let me get to the point. I don't know what happened between you and that boy, but I heard you've been walking around with a sad face for two months now. Your mom is sick of it and she's really worried about you, honey."

I sighed. Of course, it had to be my mom. She'd tried to talk to me, dragging me on a quick weekend trip with her. She'd tried shopping, pizza and drinks, but nothing had worked. Once she realized I wasn't getting out of the funk, she'd pulled in Aunt Natasha. Thankfully, my dad had been traveling on and off for the past two months and he hadn't noticed my state.

Aunt Tasha smiled at my expression and continued. "Darling, when Zain came into our lives, you'd have been way too young. You don't know what he's been through. I understand he can be closed off about his past."

I nodded, exasperated and thankful that nothing seemed to escape my big extended family. "I'm okay with 'closed off about the past'. Honestly, it's the hot and cold behavior that gets on my nerves. I mean, he cannot just walk in and out of my life whenever he feels like it. I don't care how hot he is or how sweet he was..." I broke off, unwilling to reveal too much.

Aunt Natasha placed her hand over mine. "Sweetie, would you be terribly surprised if I told you this is exactly what Arjun did to me years ago?"

"What? Uncle Arjun? No way! He adores you. I'd say he worships the ground you walk on." I've heard their love story countless times, about how Aunt Natasha fell in love with him at seventeen. It was love at first sight for her. Uncle Arjun was equally devoted to her, which is why I had a hard time believing her statement.

"Well, that wasn't always the case. I knew he was the one for me when I was seventeen, but it was several years and a lot of struggles later that we got together. Fate brought him as my bodyguard."

"Oh!" I sat forward, momentarily forgetting about my problems. This was interesting.

"Do you know why he stayed away from me all those years?"

I shook my head no.

"Because he felt he wasn't worthy of my love," she replied softly, smiling sadly at me.

"That's just a load of crap." I defended Uncle Arjun immediately.

"You and I know that darling, but men can be... umm... dense. To put it mildly." She grinned knowingly.

"Tell me about it," I grumbled.

"Well, the good news is, once we knock some sense into them, they kinda do okay."

"But how is all this connected to Zain?" I wasn't ready to make any excuses for him, not even after his thoughtful date or his out-of-this-world orgasms. Damn, I really should stop thinking about him!

"Because Zain, unfortunately, has a lot of baggage, thanks to his incompetent birth parents. I don't know how much he's told you, and I don't want to give away his secrets, but his biological mother did a number on him." Aunt Tasha broke off with a sigh. "She was an addict and put him through substance abuse, too."

"What?" My shocked gasp made her tighten her hand over mine. "I didn't... I didn't know," I whispered in agony.

"Figured as much. That's why I wanted to talk to you. To ask you to give him one more chance if you... if you truly love him."

I remained silent. I loved Zain, but I also knew he had to gain my trust.

"He's been through a lot, sweetheart, and while Mia and Armaan have done their best for that young man, sometimes, it just isn't enough. Zain must work on his healing by himself, too. Give him some time, darling. If you truly think he's the one, do this for him. For the both of you." She placed her hand on mine gently, kindness and empathy shining through her eyes.

I got up and hugged Aunt Tasha. "Thank you for telling me," I choked out, my throat thick with tears. "Perhaps I should speak to Zain."

"In that case, get going. No time like the present. What do you say?"

I hesitated for a moment before taking a deep breath. "Yes, you're right." Smiling, I kissed her cheek. "I love you, Aunt Tasha.

"Love you too, darling." She kissed my cheek before we walked out of the coffee shop together.

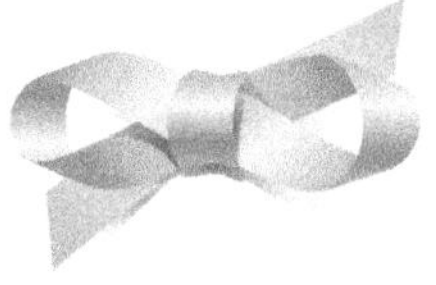

#10

Pari

The minute I disconnected the call with Aarav, I knew where I had to go. After texting my mother to let her know I'd be late, I hailed a cab to Zain's place. The entire ride was sheer torture. I couldn't get to Zain fast enough, although I had no clue what I was going to do or say once I saw him.

It had been two months since I spoke to him. In this time, he'd left me voicemails every day, talking about his day and how much he missed me. He'd sent me a book bouquet made from my favorite romantic classics and got me other gifts, which I've yet to open. I'd been a wreck the day I received the bouquet. It had taken me days to get out of my crying spree.

When I didn't respond to all this, Zain began to send me snippets of emotional and sometimes downright cheesy lines from romance books. A genre that he now apparently read. Knowing I haven't replied to a single message hasn't deterred him so far.

My heart would race with every incoming gift and message. I treasured every gift and reread his messages a thousand times. Yet, I'd been hesitant to talk to him. I was scared he would break my heart all over again.

After hearing about his life, I was truly stumped. This man, who had been repeatedly failed by his biological family, was ready to risk his heart. For me. I was ready to fight for him now.

Paying for the ride, I walked up to Zain's doorstep and rang the bell. I was pretty sure he'd be here. This was his hideout. He'd brought me here when he wanted us to have a special time. Where else would he be now? A few moments later, my hunch was proven right.

The door opened, with Zain on the other side. The air whooshed out of my lungs when I saw him stand before me in faded denim, a white button-down shirt, and bare feet. He looked messy, with his shirt partially undone and his hair unruly, as if he'd run his hand through it several times in frustration.

"Pari? Angel? What are you...? Come in!" He pulled me in before closing the door behind him.

"Hi. I wanted to talk." My cheeks felt warm, and I tried my best not to stare at his chest hair that was peeking out. My mouth turned dry. The effect he had on me the first day remained.

"Yeah, sure. Come in."

I followed him inside, plopping myself onto the huge couch. Taking a deep breath, I blurted out whatever I wanted to say without finesse. "I'm willing to give us another chance. I desperately want to. But I want you to be open and honest for this to work. Talk to me, Zain. Don't screw this up. Please."

Ignoring my outburst, he sat all too close to me, making me wiggle away. "Don't move away from me," he growled.

"Stop growling," I retorted back.

"You stop moving away from me, then," he promptly shot back.

To my utter shock, he pulled me onto his lap so that I was straddling him. "Ugh! This... this isn't how I envisioned this conversation." I hated that my voice turned all breathy. *Stupid*, I chided myself. Clearing my throat, I asked him the most obvious question first. "What happened after your mother interrupted us that day?"

Zain sighed before leaning back against the couch. "My mother," he broke off and looked away. "She was an addict, and life before I joined Mia and Armaan was devastating in a lot of ways. I was neglected. I'd gone days without food. I had no education or supervision. By the time I was ten, it was unbearable.

I stiffened, and my shocked gaze met his wary ones. "Zain. I'd no idea..." I whispered in shock. My lips trembled as my eyes automatically welled up for the small boy, for that child who had faced terrible abuse at such a young age.

"I tried my best, dammit," he growled, his hands tightening on my full hips. "I didn't want to corrupt you with my presence. I thought I could stay away, and I almost did. Until you went on a date with another man."

My body clenched at his unmistakable possessiveness, although he had no reason to be jealous. "I didn't know you were struggling so much inside." My voice cracked.

"Sweetheart, don't cry," Zain gently caressed my cheek. "I'm the selfish bastard. I couldn't let you go. Even knowing you deserved better, I couldn't give up on you. I knew it was selfish of me, yet I wanted your first kiss, your first date, your first everything." His warm breath grazed the side of my neck.

I blushed, trying not to get distracted by those memories. "We were having all that until your mother interrupted us," I recalled, desperate to get back to the issue at hand. We had to sort it out once and for all to move forward. Hopefully!

Zain nuzzled my neck, making me gasp and move my head back to give him more access. "Wait," I breathed. "We gotta talk first. Please. I lose sense of everything the minute you get close."

"Fine." He sighed before continuing, "Well, my birth mother tracked me and contacted me a couple of years ago when she discovered I was doing well in life. She wanted my money. She claimed she was clean and wanted to restart her life. Since then, she always reaches out to me if she needs money to survive." The blunt words were in direct contrast to the pain evident in his gray eyes.

"What?" That one word was filled with disbelief and anger before I took a deep breath to calm down. "I'm sorry you had to deal with that poor excuse of a human being." I gently kissed Zain on his right cheek.

"Don't be, sweetheart. She's not worth your emotions." He kissed me on my lips softly before continuing, "The other day, she landed here only to demand more money from me. When she saw you, saw that I... saw my love for you, she struck me where it hurt most."

"You love me?" I couldn't keep the wonder and awe out of my voice. The tears that had receded started again. "I don't care about anything else. I've been dying to hear it." I hugged Zain tightly, wanting him for myself. When I felt something against my ass, I wiggled. Was that his...?

"Stop moving. Not if you want to have this conversation," he groaned.

I shifted, not wanting to torture him and myself. That's when it occurred to me he'd declared his love for me. I looked at Zain, my face losing all traces of happiness. "Why the hell did you walk away if you loved me?" I demanded.

Zain smiled. "You look adorable when you're angry, like a kitten."

"Don't distract me. Answer my question first." I hit his chest, my hand hardly creating an impact against his hard muscles.

"Only because you insisted. I was petrified of the powerful feelings I had for you. When the Child protective services found out about my mother's abuse, I was eleven and a half. I was put in foster care. It was only by chance, really, that Armaan found me. One call to my mom, and they fought for my adoption. It took six months, and I was theirs."

"Wow," I whispered.

"Don't you see? I was lucky to get Mia and Armaan, but my soul is corrupted in ways you cannot even imagine. I never knew who my father was. Perhaps, a junkie who slept with my mom for his next fix, or maybe one of her boyfriends. I never knew, and she never cared to find out."

"That's terrible." The more he spoke, the harder my heart broke for him. If I'd loved Aunt Mia and Uncle Armaan before, I had a newfound respect for them now. They were angels on earth. "God forbid if I ever see that woman again..." I clenched my teeth, an unusual anger taking over me.

"Don't." His thumb brushed my lower lip. "Like I said, you're too pure for the likes of that woman." Zain leaned forward to place a soft kiss on my mouth.

I sighed. "Then don't let her affect you anymore. You deserve better. I know life hasn't been fair to you, but you have so many in your life who love you, Zain. We want you in our lives every single day."

Zain nodded. "She worked to destroy what we had that day with a single strike. But then I can't discount what she said, angel. Like it or not, I'm the biological son of an addict. The drug abuse went on for nearly two years, and even now, I have difficulty dealing with certain situations and people. I don't do well at social gatherings."

I saw Zain swallow and hugged him. "Don't do this to yourself, Zain. Please," I whispered.

"No! You need to hear this. One of the main reasons I walked away from you was to protect you. Do you know the children of an addict have a high chance of turning into addicts themselves? I still have nightmares sometimes. I might never want to be a father. How can I put you through all this?" he asked, with a disconsolate expression on his face.

"Zain!" I hissed, looking into his gray eyes with seriousness. "I will tell you this only once, and then we're done with this topic. I love you. Yes, you! With your past, your scars, and with all your wonderful, annoying traits. You. Deserve. Happiness." I punctuated each word with a soft kiss.

"Not at the cost of yours. You deserve someone who is better. Someone who would give you a better life. You're young. You might want different things down the line."

My heart went out to him when I realized he'd done this for me. But after being apart from him the last two months, I knew I'd never be able to love anyone else the way I loved Zain.

Looking into Zain's stormy eyes, I spoke earnestly, hoping he'd hear me. "Give me a better life? Even if you're the one for me?" My lips trembled. "None of us can predict the future, but let me tell you this. We will work together towards your healing. In the future, if we end up having children, they'll be a part of a very loving family. They'll be protected and cherished and would never fall prey to such abuse. I promise."

I halted when I realized what I'd said. Children? I gulped. Oh my god! Kill me! Here he was, afraid of even basic commitment, and I had to open my big mouth and talk about forever. Worse, kids!

"I didn't mean..."

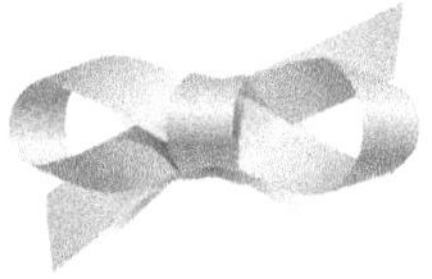

Zain

I cut her words off with a kiss. My girl had a huge heart that could hold us both together. Looking at her expression and conviction, I was hopeful for the first time in a long time. "I love you, too, my angel. You deserve so much better than me, but I am one selfish bastard. I want you. I want a future with you. Maybe, even children someday." I looked into her dazed eyes, my heart bursting with love. With her flushed cheeks and dreamy eyes, she smiled at my words.

I didn't wait for her to come down from her high. Going for the kill, I pushed her back on the couch and slid on top of her in one smooth move. Standing outside my door, clad in a peach-colored dress, she'd looked ripe and good enough to eat. I nuzzled her neck, smiling when she giggled faintly. It soon turned into a moan after my teeth scraped her soft skin.

That's when I stopped and got up almost clumsily. "Wait, I don't want to do this here. I want you in my bed. Your first time should not be on a couch; you deserve better than that." Apart from desire, I sensed panic in her eyes. "Sweetheart, do you want me to stop? All you have to do is tell me. You know that, right?"

She wiggled before sitting up. "No, I want this, but I'm a little nervous, too," she whispered.

I smiled before kissing her gently. "Don't be. If you want me to stop, all you gotta do is tell me. I'll wait until you're sure.

Yeah?" When she nodded, I got up and lifted her bridal style. She automatically put her hands around my neck as I walked toward the master bedroom.

"Wow," I heard her softly exclaim the minute I stepped into my bedroom. Done in shades of gray, I knew the room emanated masculinity. I wanted the room to be sparse and functional, and my designer achieved that with the king-size bed, a bedside table, and a couch. I gently lowered her beside the bed before pulling her into my arms for another scorching kiss.

"Umm, Zain…" I saw my angel tuck a strand of her silky hair behind her ear. "I didn't know we were, you know, going to…" she trailed off before shrugging.

I looked on, patiently waiting for her to finish. She didn't disappoint me. After a few seconds, she mustered the courage to continue. Only, it almost made me light-headed, with all the blood rushing south toward my dick.

"What I'm trying to say is… umm… I didn't come prepared. I don't have condoms or anything. And I'm not on birth control…" I saw her cheeks flush in embarrassment before she ducked her head.

She didn't realize how precious she was. I swallowed, hoping I wouldn't lose control and hurt her soft, untried body. I knew my breaking point wasn't far off. Gathering all my control, I pulled her body flush with mine and kissed her again, this time deepening the kiss, showing her I wasn't stopping for anything or anyone.

"You're precious and my forever," I murmured, before sliding my hand towards the zipper of her dress. "And you're it for me, angel. Don't worry about a single thing; I'll take care of everything." The dress pooled around her ankles as I lowered the zipper, leaving her curvy form in white cotton.

"When I meant I wasn't prepared, I meant this too," she whispered, referring to her prim underwear.

"Are you kidding me?" I groaned. "This is the sexiest thing I've ever seen." And it was. In life, simple was real. I stopped her hands from fidgeting by her sides and placed them on my shirt. "Take it off."

I felt her hands shake before she undid the buttons and took off my shirt. As if she couldn't help herself, she touched me almost reverently, tracing the tattoo on my chest. "Love this," she declared in a breathy whisper before kissing the ink. When I hissed, her head snapped up, her expression hesitant and worried.

"You can play later. It's my turn now." I walked her back to the bed before pushing her onto the huge mattress. Holding her ankle gently, I kissed her toes, sucking each one until she moaned in desperation. Only then did I trail my lips up her legs to her thighs. When my beard scraped the soft skin of her inner thighs, I felt her freeze for a second before arching up.

I smiled. My angel was more than ready for me, her nervousness from before having vanished. I looked up to find her head thrown back, her sinful lips parted. With a growl, I tore the cotton in a single move and kissed her wet heat.

"Zain!"

Her wanton gasp did nothing to curb my desire. Seeing her on my bed, at last, had broken my control. I'd fantasized about this moment so many times over the last two months. Bending down to taste her, I rejoiced in the sounds that came out of her mouth. When Pari's whimper got louder, I added my fingers, skillfully playing her body like an instrument.

Unlike in the past, where I'd never enjoyed going down on a woman much, I truly enjoyed tasting Pari, enjoying her pure, unfiltered response. I ignored the throbbing in my pants and concentrated on pleasuring my woman. Mine! Just as I felt her arousal peak, her hands pried me away from her center.

"Wait, I want you inside me," Pari panted, trying to curtail me.

"Not so fast. Come for me, angel," I growled, going back to brushing my thumb over her nub. When I bent down to take a long swipe, she came down with a breathy moan. I knew she'd thank me after her body realized this would make it easier for her to take me.

Immediately, I went up to kiss her, letting her taste herself on my lips. Looking into her eyes, I said those three words that meant the world to me now. "I love you."

Barely noticing her nod, I kicked off my jeans before entering her carefully. She was small compared to me, and I wasn't sure how to stop her from getting hurt. I wasn't too keen on scaring her with my size right now. Slowing down to make it easier for her, I sensed her trying to move up and take me in.

"Maybe you shouldn't move right now. I'm trying my best not to hurt you," I grit out, fearing I'd lose whatever little control I had.

"It's fine. Do it," she urged, trying to topple me with her innocent seduction.

"Pari..." I groaned.

When she kissed my neck and scraped her nails over my skin, something in me finally snapped, making me thrust into her in a single move. I froze when I heard her shaky hiss. Closing my eyes, I tried not to hate myself. "I'm sorry, baby."

"Don't be," she wheezed after a few seconds. "It's getting better. I'm fine. I think." She bit her lip to stop the distressed sound that threatened to come out.

"I could spank you for what you did," I growled.

"Oh, we should definitely try that, too," she answered with a giggle before trying to move and not wince.

Taking control, I kissed her soft and deep, building her desire little by little once again. As her muscles relaxed, I finally started moving, showing my angel what it was all about. My hands intertwined with hers, raising them above her head as I slowly deepened my strokes inch by agonizing inch. Bending down, I suckled her, simultaneously moving inside her.

When I heard her gasps and sensed her frustration, I increased my pace, moving my tongue over her peak repeatedly. She sobbed in agony, impatient to reach her destination. Watching the desperation on her face, I pulled her leg around my waist, angling my hips to hit her sweet spot.

Laving my tongue over her nipple, I bit her peak. Gently. Once. Immediately, her body spasmed, making her fall over the edge with a startled cry. Her eyes opened in shock at the convulsions, seeing the truth blaze in my eyes. She was all mine, and I was all hers. Our souls recognized each other, knowing this was forever.

"Love you," she breathed, her words setting off the hottest and longest climax of my life.

#11

Pari

"Oh my god, that was just... amazing," I breathed, unable to contain the pleasure and satisfaction that seeped out of my voice.

"Hmm," I heard Zain murmur before he pulled me into his freaking huge body. I almost yelped when my ass encountered something hard, something that poked and reawakened my senses. When I ground myself into him, he playfully slapped my ass, making me let out a mewl that was needy and full of desire.

"Stop that, you brat." Zain was more awake after my wiggling. "I'm trying to be considerate," he grunted. When I turned around and giggled, he opened one eye, making me kiss his nose. "What's funny?"

"Most often, you either grunt or growl. The only time you're partially expressive is when you—when we..." I trailed off, my cheeks heating at his look. A look that promised retribution if I continued. "Also..." I cleared my throat and continued, "Now that you've started reading romance, how do you like it?" I asked him with a cheeky grin.

Zain huffed out a laugh before drawing my hand to his lips. He kissed my knuckles gently before answering. "Holy hell, some of that shit is seriously spicy, angel. I'm going to take notes from all your favorite books. You've seen nothing yet. We've barely begun." He winked, making me swoon and melt into a puddle.

"Oh!" My face was on fire, and I squirmed, wanting it all right now. "I thought all the spice and dirty talk and... stuff happened only with book boyfriends. Boy, am I glad to know that's not the case. I assumed I was broken because I've never felt this way before." I swatted a hand on his chest when he chuckled.

"Happy to set you straight, sweetheart. You're far from broken." He tugged me closer, his lips almost touching mine. "Also, you come to me if you want any of your fantasies fulfilled. No book boyfriend can compete with me. Ever." He smirked.

"Can we start right now?" I asked with a pout.

Zain kissed me. "Stop tempting me, you minx. You're likely to be sore. Get up before I take you again and make it difficult for you."

I smiled at Zain's pseudo stern growl and kissed his cheek. Before I could reply, I got a text. Lazily picking up my phone, I read the text and shot up. "Oh, shit!"

"What?" He looked alarmed. Immediately, Zain got up, unabashedly naked.

That's when I saw him properly. My eyes widened and snapped to his gray ones. "How did that... that thing fit in me? Thank heavens, I was drunk with pleasure the previous night. No way would I have said okay to that if I'd looked properly!" I pointed my finger to his erection, my breaths coming out in short gasps.

When I heard Zain laugh silently, I glared at him. "Stop laughing. Ugh!" I threw a pillow at him before getting up with the sheet wrapped around me. Shaking my head, I remembered the text. "I completely forgot about my lunch with Kiara. She's in town this weekend. I forgot about my plans with her for today. I have two hours to get home, shower, change, and meet her." The words were tumbling out of my mouth even as I began to hunt for my clothes.

Zain pulled me into his arms and kissed me softly. "Hey, slow down. Your clothes are over here." He pointed to my clothes that were neatly folded on the couch. "You freshen up while I shower in the other room. I'll take you home and drop you off to meet your friend."

"Thank you." I smiled before I hurried to grab my clothes.

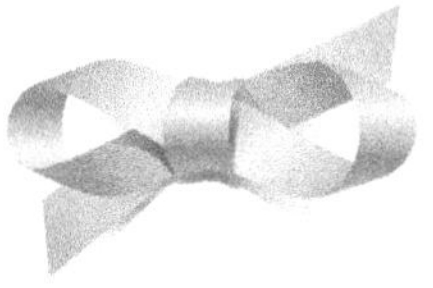

Zain

I watched my angel's retreating back and couldn't help but grin. My world had suddenly become bright, colorful, and worth living. After years, I felt something loosen up in my chest. Even with my adopted family, I've never felt this intense connection. The abuse in my formative years had unconsciously darkened a part of my soul. A part that was dormant, threatening to rear its ugly head anytime.

But my angel smashed that dark part with her radiant smile and unconditional love. She made everything seem so effortless. For the first time in my life, I felt worthy of love. Her love. Of course, I was very well aware I didn't deserve her, but I damn well was going to ensure I worked to be the man she deserved. With a smile, I went to the other room to shower and make some coffee for the both of us.

"Here you go." Fifteen minutes later, I handed her a steaming cup of coffee while she pulled her hair into a loose ponytail. That's when she noticed the mark on the side of her neck.

"Zain!" she hissed, pointing to the hickey.

I chuckled with a shrug, while her face turned red. "If you think I'm going to apologize, dream on. I love marking you, baby."

Pari rolled her eyes at me, although the hitch in her breath gave away her response to my words. "As romantic as it sounds, I'd prefer your caveman moves to be less conspicuous."

"Keep up that sarcasm and we will know how you feel about spanking," I murmured, enjoying the heat that entered her eyes. I tucked away her reaction, waiting to use it at the right time.

"I'm not getting into that discussion now. Also, my dad will kill you if he notices. Anyway, we need to leave. Pronto!"

Ignoring the comment about her father, I got up. "Let's go then." I grabbed her purse and pulled her out of my place, leading her towards my SUV. "Breakfast on the way?"

She put on her seat belt and shook her head no. "I can't eat anything right now. I'm just... full." When I smirked, she hit me on my arm. "Oh, get your mind out of the gutter."

When I laughed, she huffed but smiled as I eased the car into traffic.

. . ⁂ . .

"THIS IS THE RESTAURANT, right?" I parked the car and took off my sunglasses. Pari was seated next to me, almost vibrating with excitement. We'd gone to her place and I waited until she showered and changed. She was seeing Kiara after months and couldn't stop talking about it throughout the ride.

"Yes! Oh, I'm so looking forward to seeing Kiara. You must come too. I'd love to introduce you to her."

"Kiara?" I frowned. "Wasn't she the one who encouraged you to date?"

My angel sighed. "You know, it's high time you stopped growling. You're the only man I'm interested in and the only one for me." She ran a finger around my lips suggestively.

"I love where you're going with this." I leaned in for a kiss. To my disappointment, my angel backed away after placing a quick kiss on my lips.

"Come on, now. Let's get going."

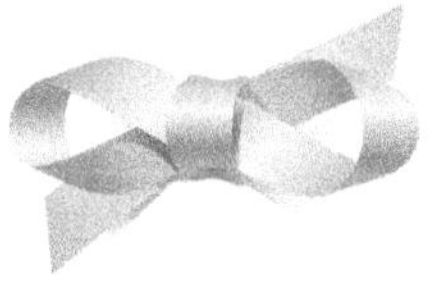

#12

Pari

I placed the fork on my plate and stared at my beautiful friend, who was hopping mad. At twenty-three, she was someone who I looked up to and aspired to be. Kiara was an outspoken, bold woman who achieved her goals once she set her mind to it. And my stunning friend was now freaking mad because her boss was an asshole. I momentarily forgot to eat and listened to her as she ranted on.

"Can you imagine the nerve of that man? Just because I am an intern, he cannot treat me like I'm an imbecile. Who does he think he is?"

"Whoa, whoa! Wait. How long have you been working for this guy? And is he the old, patriarchal type who thinks all young people are stupid?"

"I wish! This chauvinistic asshole is in his thirties, and he's just... he's too much! Frankly, there are days when I seriously consider poisoning his coffee. Or murdering him while he's attending a meeting."

I looked at Kiara in fascination. This was the first time my friend was animated about a man. I silently wondered if she was protesting a little too much. "Well, why don't we forget about your annoying boss for a while and enjoy ourselves?"

"I really want to do that. Usually, I confide in Dad, but what if he came to my workplace and interfered? My career would go down the drain even before it took off." She sighed. "Believe me, I don't want that."

I chuckled at her horrified look but understood her concerns. Her dad was Uncle Arjun's partner. An ex-army man, Kiara's father was deeply protective of his daughter, especially after Kiara's mom passed away. "Well, I have something to take your mind off your boss."

"Really? What?" That's when she noticed the love bite on my neck. Kiara gasped before whispering, "Oh my god, is it what I think it is?" She gestured towards my neck.

I nodded and blushed as she eagerly leaned forward. "Spill! Who is it? Do I know him? I'm so happy for you. Hang on, should I be happy for you?"

I laughed at her remark just as Zain walked in after finishing a call from one of his clients. He'd asked me to go ahead while he attended to the call. "Yes, you can be happy, and my boyfriend is here."

On cue, Zain stepped forward and held out his hand. Kiara shook his hand and looked at him for a few seconds before she nodded at me in approval. I heaved a sigh of relief. It meant a lot to me that Kiara approved. We sat down to continue our lunch with Zain.

• • ❧ • •

TWO HOURS LATER, I put on my seat belt while Zain reversed the car and eased onto the road. "So, did your best friend approve? I hope she doesn't feed you with any other ideas. Like dating other men..."

"Oh, for God's sake, let it go. She knows you're the one for me."

"I think I like the sound of that, angel."

I almost melted when Zain kissed my knuckles. "Anyway, she's got her own man problems now." I shrugged.

"Really?" Zain snuck a glance at me before looking forward again.

"Yep! Looks like she's having a hard time with her hot Italian boss at her new workplace. Although she claims she wants to kill him, I do sense some sparks underneath, you know?"

Zain smiled and shook his head. "As long as she doesn't take you from me, I don't care."

"As if anyone could do that. Now, take me back to your place. I already texted my mom that I won't be home before dinner."

Zain wolf-whistled. "Baby, that gives us hours. I am gonna keep you thoroughly occupied."

"I'm looking forward to that." I grinned cheekily.

Within fifteen minutes, Zain parked the car in front of his place. "Come on, angel."

"Zain, hold on for a sec. We... we need to tell your parents and mine that we're... we're dating." I hated that I sounded hesitant about us, but I wasn't sure what label our relationship had.

Zain looked at me seriously. "Sweetheart, you're my everything. If you want us to tell them right away, I'm okay. If you want to wait a while, that's okay with me, too. You know I'm gonna put a ring on your finger, right? And I'm not asking you," he hastened to add before I could cut in.

I rolled my eyes at his smirk. "You better ask me, Zain!"

"In that case, be prepared to say yes to my question."

"Always." I kissed Zain softly, thankful we found our way to each other.

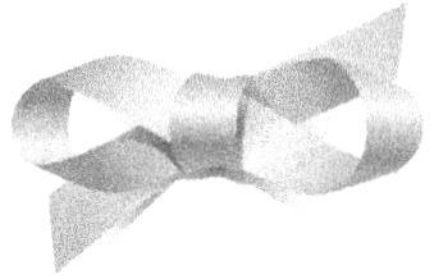

Epilogue
Two Months Later
Zain

It was time, and my palms were sweating. I was pacing my room, a little nervous about the upcoming dinner. It was time to make my relationship official, and that wasn't the reason for my nervousness. It was getting Uncle Neil's and Uncle Arjun's approval.

Every time I'd spoken to Pari or sat next to her at the dinner table at her parents', Uncle Neil watched me like a hawk. If I touched her causally in his presence, I was on the receiving end of his frosty glare. Sighing, I hoped I wouldn't have to go through a whole win-the-father-in-law spree.

Luckily, Aunt Tanya, my mom, and the other two aunts knew about us and were more than okay with Pari and me dating. Thanks to Pari's pleas, they'd kept our relationship a secret from Pari's dad, my dad, Uncle Arjun, and Uncle Rahul. We knew the men would demand I make an honest woman out of Pari immediately. Again, I didn't have any issue with that, but my angel wanted some time.

When she'd asked me for some time, I immediately wanted to protest, but I understood. She wanted to experience being in love, dating, having a boyfriend, and all the other frills before making it official. However, convincing my stupid heart wasn't easy. Every time I dropped her off at home, a little piece of my heart went with her. I hated not having her at my place as my lawfully wedded wife. Funny to think I was the one who'd been afraid to commit. Now the tables had turned, and how.

Nevertheless, thanks to these two months, I could redesign and get my house—correction, our home—ready for her to move in. I smiled when I remembered how much she'd enjoyed decorating our place. I was tempted to buy another place just to make her happy. Perhaps I would, as a wedding gift.

Wedding! I better get my act together. Straightening my collar and fixing my hair, I pocketed the ring and went down.

"Hi, honey. Are you okay?" My mom looked radiant. Along with the aunts, she'd arranged for the dinner at my parents' place.

"Yes." I cleared my throat before kissing her cheek. "I'm just a little nervous about Uncle Neil, to be honest."

"Oh, don't worry, honey. He'll come around. As long as you have Tanya on your side, you don't have to worry about a thing."

My mom had a point. Aunt Tanya knew how to make Uncle Neil say yes. All she had to do was look at him and he was putty in her hands. After Pari, I understood why. It was the same for me with her. All she had to do was give me a pleading look, and I was ready to slay the world for her.

"Anyway, do you have the ring ready?"

"Yes, Mom."

I felt my dad clap my shoulder and turned around. "Hey, Dad."

"I'm so proud of you, Zain, and I couldn't be happier about you and Pari. I always told Neil she was ours. Now it has become real, thanks to you, my son."

"You knew?"

"I have eyes," he retorted dryly, raising a brow and his glass in salute. "Fair warning, Neil might not be too happy about you snatching his baby girl." My dad smirked when I cursed silently.

"I'll work on it," I promised with a sigh.

"Don't tease my son." My mom swatted my dad's chest and gave him a kiss.

Seeing them so much in love, even after years of being married, I knew I'd made the right decision. My angel was it for me, and it was time to take the next step.

The doorbell rang just then, breaking up our little group. My parents moved forward to welcome our extended family as I checked my pocket one last time before walking forward to welcome my angel and her parents.

Pari

I stepped into Uncle Armaan's place and knew this time it was different. My eyes automatically looked for Zain and saw him walking towards the door, looking devastating in a black shirt and pants. He looked good enough to eat with his neatly trimmed beard and his muscular body. My breath automatically hitched when I remembered our lovemaking the previous evening.

One moment I'd been browsing some sites for bedsheets, and the next thing I knew, he had me on the bed. He'd had me on all fours, eating me and keeping me on edge for an hour. In the end, I had begged, pleaded, and cursed before he gave in. When he'd entered me from behind, I'd almost felt my soul leave my body.

Realizing I was blushing around my family, I hurriedly looked away and took deep breaths. I smiled when I heard Zain's mom welcome us.

The sound of car doors closing made us look back. Uncle Arjun and Uncle Rahul were walking towards the entrance along with their wives and children. Before I knew it, the room turned boisterous with greetings and hugs.

An hour later, I wasn't so sure what was happening. Aunt Mia had invited all of us, stating it was a special occasion. I wondered if it was a deal that Zain's dad had closed. Or maybe something else?

What I didn't expect was for Zain to get up to make a toast. The room fell silent as all of us looked at Zain expectantly.

"Thank you all for coming, especially at such a short notice." He looked at Uncle Rahul, who was now the Minister of External Affairs and an extremely busy man. I saw Uncle Rahul smile and nod at Zain, silently raising his glass. "Well, I wanted all of you here to make this moment special for me. For us."

My eyes widened as he looked at me. I gaped as he cleared his throat and continued. Sitting up, I held my breath, guessing what was coming next. Could it be?

"I couldn't be more thankful for life giving me a wonderful set of parents. For all that fate delivered in my younger years, life has more than made up for it after I joined you all. My mom and dad have given me everything I could possibly need, and I'm ever so grateful to them. Love you, Mom. Love you, Dad. You too, my brother." He smiled at Aarav.

I swallowed even as I saw the ladies sniffling and discreetly wiping their tears.

"But that isn't the only reason I'm grateful today. Thanks to my parents and this family, I met the love of my life. My soulmate. My forever."

As I watched Zain place his drink on the table, my mouth opened in shock.

"I don't want to wait another day before we announce to the family and the world that you're mine. Pari, my angel, will you be mine forever? Will you marry me and put me out of misery?"

I didn't realize I was crying until I wheezed, "Yes!"

Immediately, Zain put on the solitaire ring he'd gotten me and pulled me in for a kiss. "Thank you. I'm the happiest man in the world," he declared, making me smile through my tears.

We jumped apart as my mom and aunts fawned over us. Only then did we notice Uncle Arjun and my dad staring at Zain, unsmiling.

"Daddy?" I tore myself off from Zain and walked towards my dad.

"I still think it's too soon for you to get married and you should wait for a couple of years." He remained unsmiling.

"Fat chance! She belongs to us now. My son has officially claimed her with the ring," Uncle Armaan intervened before Uncle Arjun could kill Zain with a look.

"Ask your son to keep his hands to himself. I'll think about the marriage then," my dad growled while Uncle Arjun nodded in support.

Relaxing at Uncle Armaan's intervention, I finally giggled, knowing my dad and Uncle Arjun would come around. Eventually. Maybe. If Zain didn't touch me in their presence.

• • ❧ • •

"I'M GLAD I'LL LIVE to marry you. Between your dad and Uncle Arjun, I didn't think I'd come out alive," Zain murmured with a kiss.

"Shut up." I giggled. We were back at his place, champagne in our hands, snuggling on the comfortable beige couch. The ring sparkled on my hand, and I admired it one more time, unable to believe he'd planned the entire dinner, the proposal, and everything so beautifully.

For someone who had a hard time opening up, Zain had stepped out of his comfort zone, and how! If I had any doubts at all, which I didn't, it vanished at his heartfelt speech. I sighed and burrowed into his chest after draining my glass.

We had all Face-timed my brother, who was doing his undergrad at Caltech. I'd also called Kiara immediately after, wanting to let my bestie know everything. I placed the glass on the table and turned to snuggle into Zain's chest.

"For the proposal alone, you deserve a demo of a scene from my latest read," I murmured into his ear. It was no secret that I loved to read smut. Zain openly encouraged it, knowing he'd directly benefit from the results of my reading.

"Fuck," he murmured, making me bite my lip. I could feel his bulge against my stomach at my words.

I shivered before sliding down his body. "I really want to do this," I exclaimed softly, my hands hurriedly tearing the buttons of his shirt open before pulling it out of his slacks. When my hands moved to the buttons of his slacks, I felt him still.

"No!"

I knew why he said that. I'd tried giving head once, and it didn't go well. My jaw had locked, and it had hurt like hell. Well, he wasn't exactly small, and I hadn't known enough to take it slow. The result had been Zain forbidding me to go down on him ever since.

It had been okay for a couple of weeks until my aches had completely subsided. But lately, I'd wanted to give him the same pleasure he gave me. I'd read enough about it and had even spoken to Kiara, who'd helped me with some tips. Now, I wanted him in my mouth. Lockjaw be damned.

"Please. I promise I'll stop if it hurts," I begged, pulling the zipper down slowly.

"I'm not sure..." Zain gritted out, his fists clenching when I pulled his slacks and briefs down to see him already aroused.

Not bothering with a reply, I bent down to take him in my hand, slightly worried when my fingers didn't enclose his girth. Taking a deep breath, I remembered what I'd read and licked from the underside to the tip, eliciting a deep groan.

Feeling excited, I continued with little licks and hand movements, avoiding taking him fully until he cursed and caught the hair at the nape of my neck. "Suck me. Now."

A thrill ran through my body at his hoarse command. Finally, I took him in my mouth, humming at the pleasure that went through my body at the experience of taking him in my mouth. I'd been dying to taste him, and it had been nearly two months. Slowly, with caution, I moved my head, taking care to take him a little deeper with each repetition.

Through this, I felt him holding on to his control. He repeatedly asked me if I was okay, praising me and encouraging me to take it slow and deep.

"You're so good at this, angel. My God, I love it. Do that more." His praise and obvious pleasure encouraged me to lick and taste him however I deemed fit. I added my hands to the base of his length, using my tongue and mouth alternatively to bring him to the brink of release.

When I hummed once again with him in my mouth and lightly caressed him, he stilled before finishing in my mouth. Surprised but quickly swallowing, I moved my head to look up at him.

My heart warmed to see Zain looking at me with utter devotion and awe. "Holy shit! If this is what reading does, I want to build a library for you."

I giggled and groaned softly when Zain flipped me beneath his body. "Time to return the favor." He declared with a boyish smile, making me fall in love with him all over again. He ravished me thoroughly, ensuring I came multiple times before he relented. I sighed dreamily. "I love you. A lot."

Zain gently kissed me before pulling me into his arms, engulfing me in a tight hug. "Me too, my angel, always and forever. Thank you for coming into my life, for not giving up on me," he whispered with a smile.

I kissed his chest and smiled back, looking forward to the next sixty years or more with this man. He was my perfect book boyfriend come to life and my path to our happily ever after. With my love by my side, I knew life would be perfect. And it was!

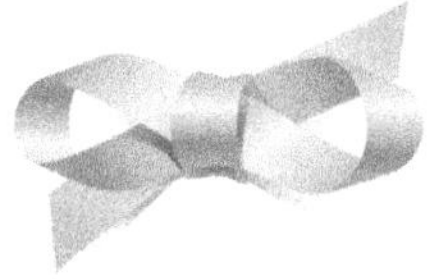

Bonus Scene
Zain

"**P**ari! Angel, where are you?" I growled, closing the ornate door after me hurriedly. She had rented a cozy home stay for the holidays that I now entered with my bag. I was impatient to see my wife, and the closer I got to her the more impatient I turned. After tying up all the loose ends in Bangalore, I was supposed to join my wife in Hyderabad, where she'd already started her masters two months ago. With the slight delay in wrapping my projects, it had taken me two extra months to join my wife.

The resulting long-distance relationship left me frustrated and grumpy, a fact that didn't go unnoticed by my staff or my family. Every time I'd become unbearable, they'd either FaceTime my angel or ask me to get the hell out to meet my wife. Sadly, the past month had been really hectic, leaving me more growly and frumpy than usual.

Finally, I'd been all set to get onto a flight to Hyderabad. I'd been confused and thrown off when the tickets to Kashmir had instead landed in my inbox last night. My angel had planned this holiday all by herself, keeping the entire thing a suspense until the last moment. Immediately, I perked up, counting each second until I could see my sunshine once again. I missed her touch, her body, her scent, her smile; in short, everything about her.

When I'd landed in Kashmir, I'd been thrilled to see the snow everywhere. Pari loved the holiday season. She loved a white Christmas in particular, insisting the snowflakes added magic to the air.

I smiled, thinking about my girl, who loved to see everyone happy. This season gave her exactly that, celebrations and cheer all around. As for me, I didn't mind it as long as my angel was next to me.

When I didn't see Pari in the living room, I frowned, taking two stairs at a time. She knew I was on the way, yet she wasn't around. Where the hell was my woman? I was all set for barging into the bedroom when I halted. Standing by the doorway of the bedroom was my angel.

"Fuck!" The bag fell from my hands with a thud. I stared at the vision in front of me, my body instantly reacting to the sight of the sexiest elf I'd seen in my life. Wearing a strapless elf costume with thigh high socks, Pari looked insanely hot.

With a roar, I pushed Pari into the bedroom, following her clumsily. I didn't give her any time to react or move, grounding my lips to hers before she could take another step.

"Are you trying to drive me crazy, angel? You know what happens whenever I've been denied you. Yet you tease me like this," I growled, biting her lips. "I love what you're wearing. Hell, I've missed you. I've missed this," I bit her neck before suckling the same spot gently.

I heard Pari's breath hitch before she let out an answering breathy moan. "Surprise."

"Best fucking surprise ever." My hands tugged hard at the string that held the strapless top in place. Immediately, the material gave away, leaving her round, cherry-tipped breasts bare to my lust-filled gaze. Bending down, I captured one peak in my mouth while my other hand directly sought her heat.

I murmured in satisfaction when I heard Pari moan. Her legs trembled the minute my fingers encountered bare flesh. I cursed, thrilled and aroused at her naughty costume. As always, my perfect wife was enacting another bookish fantasy of hers.

Only this morning had she sexted me some phrases of her latest read, a Christmas smut. Now, she was acting on the fantasy, making me the luckiest man alive. Giving her no time to act further, I plunged my finger into her wet heat, making her cry out my name.

"Zain!" I heard her cry, my fingers immediately getting drenched.

"You little tease, enticing me like this." My fingers scissored inside her, wanting to drive her crazy with want and need. When her inner muscles clenched, I knew I was getting there.

"Ah, Zain, I'm close..." Pari caught my biceps, trying to stand upright.

At her words, I immediately withdrew my hands.

"Zain!" Pari cried, frustrated that I stopped.

"Not so fast, angel. You made me wait for one entire month. Maybe you can wait for a few more minutes."

"I swear I'm going to kill you," Pari whined in a breathless voice.

I chuckled at her cute little elf face, now filled with annoyance. I carried her to the bed and placed her on the mattress on all fours. Stepping back, I noticed her short dress barely covering her, leaving her juicy bits to my mercy.

I steadied my breath at the erotic sight in front of me and hoped I didn't come before I could have my way with her. Circling her hip with one hand, I caressed her bare cheek with the other, enjoying the smooth skin that had turned pink in the past. But today wasn't that day. Today, I wanted to drive her crazy with want. For me. Only for me.

"Zain, please," Pari wriggled, causing my dick to almost explode.

I swore and pulled her hip towards me before bending down to taking a long swipe at her wet heat. I murmured in satisfaction at her taste, enjoying the flavors one more time. I'd missed this, missed touching and tasting my angel. Thankful the wait was finally over, I tasted my gift, lapping up the juices with an enthusiasm that bordered on obscene.

"Oh, my God. I love this, I love you. I missed you." Pari caught the sheet with her hand as she trembled in my arms.

I paused, my heart filling with warmth and something sweet at her confession. I'd never tire of hearing her tell me she loved me. I lived for her. I lived for this. Instead of answering back, I preferred to show her, this time attacking her clit with my tongue. When my fingers joined in, I felt her splinter apart in my arms with a sharp cry.

Standing up, I quickly adjusted my clothes and got into her from behind before she got down from her post orgasmic high. I entered her in a single thrust, enjoying the snug feeling. "Fuck, I missed this connection with you, angel. No more long distance." I growled, done with being apart from Pari.

"I'll agree to anything if you move right now," she answered, wriggling her ass. The minx!

I moved then, slowly at first, before picking up the pace steadily. With her elf costume half undone and her socks intact, she was a wet Christmas dream come true. When one of her hands moved between her legs, I was done.

Spanking her ass once, I moved hard and fast, chasing my completion and my angel's. I moved her fingers from her core and replaced them with mine. When I pinched her and slammed into her all at once, I felt her convulse around me for the second time within minutes.

The rhythmic pulsing triggered my own climax, and I stilled in her with a hoarse cry. A few minutes later, I carefully dislodged myself from Pari and dropped onto the bed. Pulling her to my sated body, I kissed the back of her neck. "Happy fucking Christmas, angel," I murmured.

"Merry Christmas to you, too, my love."

Her sweet voice and her smile made me turn her around. I kissed the tip of her nose, thankful I have her in my life. "Thank you for putting up with me, angel. I love you."

"I love you too, honey, and the pleasure is all mine. Literally."

We both burst out laughing at her pun. Snuggling her into my warm body, I kissed her forehead, thankful we had each other as we rode the sunset together.

Do you want to read Kiara and her hot Italian boss, Alessandro's, 'Billionaire

Office Romance'? Check out CHEESY LOVE.

. . ⸙ . .

ABOUT THE AUTHOR

Dee James is a contemporary romance author whose books have consistently featured in the Bestseller Lists on Amazon India.

Apart from coffee, makeup, and her balcony garden, Dee loves to write quirky, innocent, and curvy heroines who find their happily ever after with sinful-looking, growly billionaires. Sweet and steamy, her romance novellas are peppered with passionate and swoon-worthy moments. If you're looking for low-angst, feel-good romantic reads with a guaranteed HEA, you're in the right place!

. . ⸙ . .

To get exclusive updates on Dee's upcoming releases, access her freebies & bonus scenes, and to receive free steamy recommendations, subscribe to Dee's Newsletter – ***Dee James' Romance Reads n Recos in Substack.***

CONNECT WITH DEE VIA

DEE JAMES' ROMANCE READERS' GROUP (Facebook)

INSTAGRAM[1] (https://instagram.com/ authordeejames)

---

1. https://www.instagram.com/authordeejames/

Don't miss out!

Visit the website below and you can sign up to receive emails whenever Dee James publishes a new book. There's no charge and no obligation.

https://books2read.com/r/B-A-BXTV-YCMDC

BOOKS 2 READ

Connecting independent readers to independent writers.

Also by Dee James

Curvy & Decadent
Fiery Love
Cheesy Love
Spicy Love
Crazy Love
Curvy Love
Married Love

Watch for more at https://authordeejames.substack.com/about.